A not-so-excellent vacation

STEPHANIE

Stephanie is looking forward to vacationing at the Hawaiian Hideaway—a totally fancy hotel. She can't wait to take hula lessons—the ones her hotel offers for free! Too bad Danny made reservations at the *Hideaway Haven Hotel*. There's not even a pool at this place! Not to mention, no hula lessons.

Then Stephanie is mistaken for a guest of the Hawaiian Hideaway Hotel! She quickly signs up for the free dance lessons—hula, here she comes! But can Stephanie keep her secret? Or is she headed for hula trouble?

MICHELLE

Michelle loves the Hideaway Haven Hotel. Staying in a hut and exploring a tropical rainforest is totally excellent! It's like Michelle's own jungle adventure!

But the adventure gets a little *too* real when Michelle finds out she's disturbed an evil spirit! Which means she's cursed! If she can't find a way to stop the curse by the full moon, something terrible will happen!

Will Michelle find the cure for the curse? Or is she totally doomed?

FULL HOUSE™: SISTERS books

Available from MINSTREL Books

FULL HOUSE™
Sisters

Problems in Paradise

DEBORAH PERLBERG

A Parachute Press Book

A
MINSTREL®
BOOK

Published by POCKET BOOKS
New York   London   Toronto   Sydney   Singapore

A MINSTREL PAPERBACK *Original*

A Minstrel Book published by
POCKET BOOKS, a division of Simon & Schuster Inc.
1230 Avenue of the Americas, New York, NY 10020

A PARACHUTE PRESS BOOK

Copyright © and ™ 1999 by Warner Bros.

FULL HOUSE, characters, names and all related indicia are trademarks of Warner Bros. © 1999.

ISBN: 0-671-04057-X

First Minstrel Books printing December 1999

10 9 8 7 6 5 4 3 2 1

A MINSTREL BOOK and colophon are registered trademarks of Simon & Schuster Inc.

Printed in the U.S.A.

Chapter
1

"Hawaii is a land of crashing surf and majestic palm trees,'" Stephanie Tanner read aloud from the guidebook. "'Imagine yourself walking along a white beach under a glorious sunset. . . .'"

She peered through the airplane window at the green islands below. *I don't have to imagine it*, Stephanie thought. *I'm going to be there soon!*

She reached for the brochure that described the hotel where she and her family would spend the week. She had already read through it about a million times. But she couldn't help looking at it again.

"But did I read you this part, Michelle?" Stephanie turned to her nine-year-old sister. Michelle sat in the next seat. She was pulling a piece of folded paper out of her daypack.

"'The Hawaiian Hideaway Hotel is one of the most luxurious hotels in all the Hawaiian Islands,'" Stephanie read aloud.

Michelle grinned. "Steph, you've read that to me so many times, I've got it memorized," she said.

Stephanie leaned back in her seat and closed her eyes. "Room service, a beauty spa, attendants who serve you refreshments on the beach. We'll be waited on hand and foot. No homework, no chores—we won't have to lift a finger for one whole week!"

"I just hope I get to do everything I planned," Michelle said. She unfolded the piece of paper she had taken from her pack. It was a long, handwritten list.

Stephanie leaned over and read it out loud. "Scuba diving, snorkeling, surfing, swimming, sailboarding, sailing, hiking . . ." The list went on and on. "You really think you can fit that all into one week?"

2

"Definitely," Michelle replied.

"Just leave time for the really important stuff," Stephanie said. "Like having facials and mud packs in the hotel spa."

Michelle rolled her eyes. "You can get a facial back in San Francisco. When we're on Maui, I want to do Hawaiian-type stuff I can't do anywhere else. I just need someone to do it with me."

"No problem," Stephanie told her. "With this group, you're bound to find someone who's interested."

At home in San Francisco, Stephanie, Michelle, and their older sister, D.J., shared a very full house. Years ago, when the girls' mother died, their father, Danny Tanner, needed help raising his three daughters. So his best friend, Joey Gladstone, moved in—as did the girls' Uncle Jesse. Then Jesse married Rebecca Donaldson, Danny's co-host on the TV show, *Wake Up, San Francisco.* When Jesse and Becky had twin boys, the four of them moved into the attic apartment. Now Alex and Nicky, who were four, were the youngest members of the family.

Stephanie turned around. Across the aisle her little cousins were sound asleep, taking their afternoon naps. In the seats directly behind her, her dad and her Aunt Becky were sleeping, too. They both wore black satin sleeping masks.

Michelle giggled. "Dad and Aunt Becky must be really tired. They both fell asleep before the twins did."

Stephanie sighed. "I was afraid Dad wasn't going to do anything except sleep this week. Remember when he said that on his vacation he just wanted to stay home and lie around the house?"

"Yeah. I was afraid it was going to be the most boring week ever," Michelle admitted. "I am *so* glad we convinced him to go to Hawaii instead."

"Well, he needs it," Stephanie said. "I mean, staying in a luxury hotel right on the beach is going to be the most restful vacation ever. Dad won't have to worry about a thing. It's going to be an absolutely perfect vacation for him— and for us!"

"It's too bad Joey and D.J. couldn't come

along," Michelle said. "D.J. would love that spa stuff. And I know Joey would want to go scuba diving with me."

Stephanie glanced out her window again. They were flying lower now, and she could see a strip of sparkling white beach dotted with palm trees. "Hey! We're getting closer to the island," she said.

Michelle leaned across her sister to peer out the window. "I like Hawaii already," she decided. "This vacation is going to be totally perfect."

"It's *got* to be," Stephanie told her, "if we ever want Dad to let us help plan a vacation again."

Stephanie smiled to herself, remembering how Danny had asked for her input on where she'd like to stay. There was no competition in Stephanie's mind—the Hawaiian Hideaway was *the* place to be on Maui.

Moments later the wheels of the plane touched down on the runway. "Aloha. Welcome to the island of Maui," a flight attendant said. "The temperature here is a comfortable eighty-six degrees."

When the plane taxied to a stop at the terminal, Stephanie released her seat belt and got to her feet. Other passengers pulled their luggage from the overhead bins. They were all talking and laughing, eager to get off the plane. Only Danny and Becky were still asleep.

How can anyone sleep through all this commotion? Stephanie wondered. She reached back to the seats behind her. She gently shook her father's shoulder. "Wake up, Dad. Wake up, Aunt Becky," she called. "We're in Hawaii!"

Stephanie stepped out of the terminal and took a deep breath. The air was warm and fragrant with the scent of tropical flowers. The sun was bright, the sky was absolutely cloudless. Perfect.

Danny frowned. He glanced left and right. "Somewhere around here, we're supposed to find the van that will take us to our hotel," he said.

"It must be over there." Stephanie pointed to a large parking area. It was lined with vans.

Each one had the name of a hotel painted across its side.

"I don't see the one for our hotel," Danny said.

Stephanie felt a little pang of worry. "I'm sure our van is on its way," she said.

"Hula dancers!" Nicky suddenly shouted.

Everyone turned to look. Beside the main terminal, four young women swayed to the music of a Hawaiian guitar. They wore grass skirts and leis of colorful flowers.

Nicky sprinted off. "I want to see the hula girls!"

"Me, too!" Alex yelled. He darted after Nicky.

"Hey, you guys—come back here!" Jesse dropped the suitcases he was carrying. He took off after the twins, and Becky took off after Jesse.

"Stephanie—you and Michelle stay here and watch our bags," Danny called as he ran after all of them.

Stephanie heard the roar of engines starting in the parking area. One by one, the hotel vans pulled away.

"Uh-oh." Michelle's blue eyes widened. "They all left. Without us."

"It's okay. None of them was our van," Stephanie explained.

"Well, where do you think *our* van is?" Michelle asked.

Stephanie shrugged. She was wondering the same thing.

Danny and the others started back toward Stephanie and Michelle. Stephanie glanced over at the parking area. It was still empty. No van from the Hawaiian Hideaway was in sight.

"You know something, Michelle?" Stephanie said. "I suddenly have a bad feeling about this."

"What do you mean?" her sister asked.

Stephanie studied the empty lot. "I mean, I really hope the rest of our 'perfect' vacation turns out better than this!"

Chapter
2

Stephanie's right, Michelle thought. *This is not a good start to Dad's perfect, restful vacation.*

"Look at me, Michelle!" Nicky called out. "I'm taller than everyone!"

Michelle waved at her little cousin, who was sitting on Danny's shoulders. Right behind them, Jesse and Becky led Alex by the hand.

"Whew!" Danny set Nicky down on the grass in front of Michelle. "That was a work-out. These little guys sure can run. So, where's our van? I can't wait to get to the hotel."

"Me either," Becky agreed. "I'm totally ready for that spa."

Michelle and Stephanie exchanged a very worried glance.

"Well, I hate to tell you this," Michelle began. "But our van—"

A loud beeping sound interrupted her.

"Has just arrived!" she finished. She felt a wave of relief as the van pulled into the hotel shuttle parking area. Now their vacation could begin the *right* way!

Wait a minute . . .

This van didn't look like the others. It was old and needed washing. The letters across its side were so faded, she could barely read what they said.

The van sped up to the curb and parked. A young blond boy sitting beside the driver got out. He looked about Michelle's age.

"You just found us," Michelle told him.

"Great! I'm Joe," the boy introduced himself. "My dad and I run the Hideaway Haven Hotel."

"*You* run our hotel?" Michelle raised an eyebrow. "You're a kid like me."

"He means he *helps* run the hotel," the driver said. He got out of the van and shook

10

hands with Danny. "I'm Ned Grant, Joe's dad," he told them. "I own the Haven, along with my partner, Ken Takei."

Mr. Grant was a tall, strong-looking man. He had the same blond curls and merry blue eyes as his son.

"We're not usually late to meet the planes," Mr. Grant explained. "But we ran out of gas."

"Well, accidents happen," Danny said. He glanced at the name painted on the side of the van. "But I'm a little confused. I called to make reservations at the Hawaiian Hideaway Hotel. Your van says you're from the Hideaway Haven Hotel."

"Right. The Hawaiian Hideaway is the fanciest luxury hotel in our travel brochure," Michelle added.

Mr. Grant frowned. "There must be some mistake. I have your reservation right here." He showed Danny a slip of blue paper.

Danny's cheeks flushed red. "You're right," he agreed. "I made reservations at the Hideaway Haven, not the Hawaiian Hideaway. I guess I got the names mixed up. I'm very sorry, everybody."

"Accidents happen," Mr. Grant said with a chuckle.

"You should stay with us anyway. Hideaway Haven is the best," Joe piped up. "You'll see."

Danny looked undecided for a moment. Then he smiled and shrugged. "Well, we're on vacation. So why get stressed? Sure, we'll stay at the Hideaway Haven."

"Dad," Stephanie said quietly. "Are you sure you want to do that?"

"Yeah, why not?" Danny answered. "I'm determined to be totally relaxed this whole week. The Hideaway Haven will be fine."

"Thanks, Mr. Tanner," Mr. Grant told him. "I know you'll have a great vacation with us."

"I'm sure we will," Danny said.

Michelle shook her head in disbelief. Was this her dad talking? Danny Tanner, who was fussy about everything?

He must be relaxed already, she thought.

Danny, Becky, and Jesse began handing Mr. Grant their suitcases and tote bags. Then they all climbed in, and the van pulled away.

"We'll be there in about twenty minutes," Mr. Grant said as he turned onto the highway.

Joe turned around in the front seat. "I can show you all sorts of neat things around the Haven," he offered.

"Can you show me where to hike and swim and snorkel?" Michelle asked.

"Definitely," Joe said. "I know all the best places. I'll take you to my favorite climbing trees, too."

All right! Michelle thought. Even if her whole family didn't want to do all the same things that she did, it sounded like Joe would. She'd probably get to do everything on her list by the time the week was through.

"There are tons of cool places to go," Joe went on. "Like the palm grove where the very first mainland Americans settled."

"Joe knows quite a bit about local lore," his father added.

"What's that?" Michelle asked.

"Stories," Joe replied. "I know all sorts of stories about the island's history. And local legends."

"Cool," Michelle said. She sat back and gazed out the window of the van. They drove past trees with bright tropical flowers and

1 3

cliffs cut by waterfalls. Wow! The island was paradise!

After a while, Mr. Grant turned off the main highway onto a narrow dirt road. Thick stands of trees grew on both sides. Michelle could hear the sound of ocean waves in the distance.

The van pulled into a large circular clearing. "This is it," Joe declared.

"Welcome to Hideaway Haven," Mr. Grant added.

Michelle bolted upright. *This is it?* she thought. *No way. It can't be!*

All she could see around here were a bunch of old huts!

She glanced at Joe and his dad to see if they were kidding.

Nope. Mr. Grant seemed perfectly serious— proud, even.

Michelle's family was unusually quiet. Becky blinked in surprise. Jesse raised his eyebrows. Her father stood wide-eyed. Stephanie was turning a pale shade of green. Even the twins' mouths hung open.

Which meant Michelle had to be the one to

speak up. "Are you sure this is it?" she asked Mr. Grant.

"Of course I'm sure," he replied. "Ken and I have owned this place for the last fifteen years."

"B-but—this isn't a bit like a luxury hotel," she stammered. "Not a bit!"

In fact, she thought to herself, *at first glance this place looks like a serious dump.*

Chapter
3

Stephanie stepped out of the van and gulped hard. This place didn't look like a hotel at all!

"I've got to get back to the office," Mr. Grant told them. He grinned and mussed his son's hair. "But Joe will show you to your rooms. And I'll send someone to bring in your bags."

"It's rustic but . . . kind of charming," Becky said as Mr. Grant hurried away. "Don't you think so, Steph?"

Stephanie shook her head. *Charming* was definitely not the word she would have picked for this run-down place.

1 6

Hideaway Haven was nothing more than a group of huts surrounding a clearing. They all had whitewashed walls and straw roofs.

"I've got to admit, this isn't the kind of hotel I thought I had booked," Danny said. "But you're right, Becky, it does seem to be really authentic."

"These must be like the huts the native Hawaiians built," Jesse agreed. "Totally cool."

How about totally primitive? Stephanie thought. *Not to mention depressing.* She couldn't help comparing Hideaway Haven to the Hawaiian Hideaway—the luxury hotel she'd read about in the brochure.

It did not compare well.

There was no sign of an enormous pool or a spa. No sign of well-stocked refreshment stands lining a shady beach. Wait . . . there wasn't even a single sign of a beach!

Stephanie tapped Joe's arm. "I don't suppose there's a whole part of this place we're not seeing. You know, the part with a pool, room service, cable TV, and a spa?"

Joe shook his head. "Nope. This is it."

"But the other hotel has all of those things."

Stephanie pointed at the brochure for the Hawaiian Hideaway.

"Sorry." Joe shrugged. "My dad and Ken wanted the Haven to be completely authentic," he explained. He pointed to an opening in the trees. "There's a trail through there that leads straight to the beach. But there's no pool or spa, no phones in the rooms. And definitely no TV."

"You don't have TV at *all?*" Stephanie groaned. This was even worse than she'd thought!

"Nope," Joe said. "Originally we didn't even want to have running water."

"*What?*" Stephanie shrieked. "How will I wash my hair? Or take a shower?"

Danny frowned. "No water? With the twins, that could be a problem. We—"

"Oh, don't worry—we *do* have it now," Joe assured him. "But mostly this is a very plain hotel. We like it that way."

"I don't get it," Stephanie said. "Why?"

"Because my dad and his partner wanted Hideaway Haven to be exactly what the name says," Joe explained. "A hideaway from the modern world."

18

Danny appeared thoughtful. "That's very interesting," he said.

"Well, it sure sounds . . . different," Jesse admitted.

"This is awful!" Stephanie turned to Danny and Becky. "I feel so bad for you guys. You needed this vacation more than anyone. And now we're *here*." She pointed to one of the huts.

Becky slowly nodded. "I was looking forward to being completely lazy," she admitted.

"Well, forget that," Stephanie said. "No lying around in a sauna or at a pool. No facials at the spa." She turned to her dad and spoke in a low voice. "Maybe it's not too late to book rooms at the Hawaiian Hideaway Hotel," she suggested. "They have everything we wanted there."

Danny shrugged. "Actually, I kind of like it here," he said.

"Are you sure?" Stephanie stared at him in surprise.

"It may be plain, but that might be just what we need."

"What do you mean?" Michelle asked.

1 9

"Well, there won't be any phones ringing," Danny said. "Which means no unwanted calls or interruptions."

"Hey! That's right!" Becky brightened, too. "And with no TV blaring all the time, we won't think about our own TV jobs."

"This could be exactly the kind of total, complete vacation you need," Jesse added. "Nothing but lying on the beach, reading a good book. . . ."

"And taking long naps," Becky finished for him. "Now, that sounds like paradise to me!"

"The twins only want to dig in the sand and swim in the ocean," Jesse went on. He dropped a kiss on the end of Becky's nose. "And I promise to watch the kids so you can have total rest!"

Stephanie gazed from one bare hut to the next. Her vision of a dream vacation fizzled before her eyes. She turned to her sister. Maybe Michelle would back her up.

"What do you think, Michelle? You wanted to do fancy resort stuff, too, right?" she asked her.

"I don't mind the Haven," Michelle said.

"Staying here sounds like fun. Just a different kind of fun."

"Are you okay with that, Steph?" Danny asked. "I mean, this vacation is for all of us. I want you to be happy, too."

Stephanie bit her lip. Her dad already seemed more relaxed and happy than he had been for weeks, and Becky and Jesse both seemed to like it. Not to mention Michelle.

Maybe I'm not being fair, Stephanie thought. *Even if this isn't my dream vacation, it really could be exactly what Dad and Becky need.*

There was only one thing to do. Stephanie swallowed hard, then smiled. "This will be fine," she told her dad. "After all, when in Hawaii, do like the Hawaiians do, right?"

"That's the spirit!" Danny gave her a hug.

"I'll show you your huts." Joe pulled a small pad from his back pocket and flipped through its pages. "Hmm . . . Tanner family," he said. "Stephanie and Michelle, this way."

He led them to a hut on the side of the clearing. Its door was painted a bright, cheery blue.

Stephanie was relieved to see that the hut was actually clean and airy inside. A vase of fresh flowers sat on the dresser. Someone had even set out a bowl of fresh fruit with a large glass dome over it, and a tin of crackers on the small table beneath the window.

"See, Steph? This is nice," Michelle said.

"Well, I guess it isn't *so* bad," Stephanie agreed. She flopped down on her bed. It felt totally comfy.

She glanced up at the soft white mosquito netting that hung over the bed from a hook in the ceiling. The netting was draped like a canopy. It made Stephanie think of princesses and castles.

"Mmmm," she said. She stretched out and closed her eyes. "Maybe I could get used to this!" Her hand touched something soft and fuzzy.

She turned her head and opened her eyes.

"Eeeeeaaaaah!" she screamed.

She leaped off the bed and screamed again.

"What is it?" Michelle cried in alarm. She raced to Stephanie's side.

Stephanie pointed at the bed.

A huge, hairy black spider was sitting in the middle of her pillow!

Chapter
4

Michelle leaped back from the bed. "Ugh!" she yelled. "That's the biggest, hairiest, most disgusting spider I've ever seen!"

"Watch out!" Stephanie warned. "It might be poisonous!"

Joe came running into the hut. "What's wrong?" He spotted the spider and burst out laughing.

"Hey, stop screaming," he said. "You'll scare the poor thing!"

Michelle's mouth dropped open as Joe lifted the spider in one hand and held it out toward Stephanie.

"Aaaah!" she screamed.

Joe stroked the spider's broad, fuzzy back with his finger. "This guy is just a banana spider," he explained. "He's harmless. He can't hurt anything—except bananas. See?" He shoved the spider toward Stephanie.

"I see! I see! Just get it away from me!" Stephanie squealed.

"Sorry." Joe let the spider walk along his wrist.

Wow. If Joe can be that cool about it, I can, too, Michelle thought. She reached out gingerly and touched the spider. It felt soft and fuzzy, like a powder puff.

Joe smiled at her. "See, he just wants to be friends," he said.

"Hey, Joe. Why don't you show us around a little?" Michelle suggested. "You know, to make up for scaring Stephanie."

"Sure. That would be great!" Joe said.

"Yeah," Stephanie mumbled. "Great."

Michelle had to laugh. Stephanie's face was slightly green. But she'd be okay.

Joe led Michelle and Stephanie out of the hut and through the open clearing.

"I'll go tell Dad we're going for a walk," Michelle volunteered.

She found Danny talking with Joe's dad in front of a hut with a sign that read OFFICE.

"Dad, Joe's going to show Stephanie and me around, okay?" she asked.

Danny turned to Mr. Grant. "Is it safe for the kids to be out on their own?"

"Absolutely," Mr. Grant replied. "The grounds are totally safe here. The kids can explore the Haven all by themselves."

"But don't stay away too long," Danny told Michelle. "I want to get in some good family time later."

"No problem," Michelle promised. She hurried back to join her sister and Joe. "All set!" she reported. "Let's go to the beach first."

Joe led them down a shaded path. Colorful tropical birds flew among the trees. The sound of the ocean grew louder.

A few minutes later the trail opened onto sparkling white sand. Michelle gasped. She shaded her eyes.

This was the most gorgeous beach she'd ever seen! The sand was soft and warm. The water was a bright turquoise blue. Lush palm trees edged the water. And the shoreline seemed to stretch on forever!

"Hey, this is pretty amazing," Stephanie said. She sounded surprised. And happy.

"Yeah!" Michelle agreed.

Stephanie pointed at the long, low building in the distance. "Hey. What's that?" she asked.

"That's the Hawaiian Hideaway," Joe replied. "The place you were supposed to stay."

"It is?" Stephanie peered harder.

"Yes." Joe made a face. "My dad's partner, Ken, grew up on this island," he said. "And Ken says none of the luxury stuff they have there is like the real native Hawaii."

"Right," Stephanie mumbled.

Joe pointed toward the woods behind the beach. "Come on, let's hike up that way," he said. "There's a really cool secret path I want to show you."

"Look, you guys, I'm going to bail on this tour," Stephanie told them. "I'd rather just take a little walk up the beach." She waved. "Catch you later."

Problems in Paradise

Michelle shrugged and turned back to Joe. "*I* want to see that secret path. Will you show me?" she asked.

"Sure." Joe led the way across the sand and headed back toward the woods. He pointed to an opening in the trees that was half hidden beneath low bushes.

"I discovered this path just a little while ago," he explained. "Even Ken and my dad didn't know about it."

Michelle gazed along the tree line. From where they were standing, she couldn't see the path that led back to the hotel.

"We're pretty far from the Haven, aren't we?" she asked.

"Not really," Joe replied. "I can show you where this path links to the one we took before. You just have to know where to look."

Joe ducked down under the low bushes, and Michelle followed. This trail was narrower than the first. And even more beautiful. Red and yellow flowers bloomed on thick vines that clung to the trees. Bird songs filled the air.

"Wow!" Michelle gasped.

Joe grinned at her. "Haven't you ever been in a tropical forest before?"

"Joe!" Mr. Grant's voice boomed out from the direction of the clearing. "Where are you?"

Joe glanced at his watch. "Whoops! I need to get back to the hotel. I promised to help my dad with some stuff." He turned. "I'll be right there!" he shouted back.

"I guess I'll head back, too." Michelle tried not to look as disappointed as she felt.

"No way! As long as you stay on the trail, you can go exploring on your own," Joe said.

"Really?" Michelle brightened.

"Sure. Come on." Joe hurried along the winding path. Michelle was right behind him. Suddenly he stopped in front of a large tree.

Michelle's blue eyes grew round. Either the tree had dozens of skinny trunks—or its branches were growing downward. It was the weirdest tree she had ever seen. "What *is* that?" she asked. "A mutant tree?"

"It's a banyan," Joe explained with a laugh. "Its branches grow shoots that drop to the ground and take root."

He reached into his pocket and pulled out a

bright red bandanna. He tied it around one of the lower branches.

"If you look right under this branch, you'll see that this trail meets up with the one that leads back to the hotel," Joe explained. "Take it and you'll be back at the Haven in no time."

Michelle watched as Joe headed toward the hotel. She glanced at his red bandanna on the banyan tree. Joe's directions were easy to follow. She'd have no trouble finding her way back.

She plunged into the forest on her own. The path was dark, shaded by the tall palm trees overhead. Long, loopy vines hung everywhere. *This really is kind of neat,* Michelle thought. *I'm alone in a tropical paradise!*

The path led up a steep hill. Michelle was breathing hard by the time she reached the top. She glanced around at the thick bushes that covered the top of the hill. Then Michelle caught sight of something sparkling between the leaves.

I wonder what that is? She pushed the leaves aside and ducked through.

Whoa! A swimming hole!

Michelle stared at the large, calm pool of emerald-green water. It was shaded by more overhanging vines and palm trees. Blue, yellow, and red flowers dotted the vines and trees and bushes.

I wish I could jump right in, she thought. *Wait a minute—I can!*

Michelle realized she was wearing her pink bathing suit underneath her sundress. She was really glad she had slipped her suit on that morning before she got on the plane.

Good thing I believe in being prepared! she thought.

She walked over to a wide strip of sand by the side of the pool. After pulling her sundress over her head, she set it down on a dry rock. Carefully, she stuck one foot into the water.

"Aaah! Perfect!" she said aloud. The water felt fantastic.

She waded in, swam a few strokes, then turned over and floated on her back.

Too bad Stephanie isn't here, Michelle thought. *She'd really be impressed by finding this beautiful swimming hole!*

She floated for a while in the warm sunlight

and let her eyes drift shut. *I could really get into this relaxation stuff,* she decided.

She opened her eyes with a start as she remembered—her father had said not to be gone too long.

So she climbed out of the water and pulled on her sundress again. Michelle hummed as she followed the path back down the hill. She stopped once to gather an armful of the bright tropical flowers. *These will make a perfect bouquet to decorate our hut,* she thought.

Michelle continued along the path. She soon found the banyan tree with Joe's bandanna tied on it. She freed the bandanna from the branch and started toward the hotel.

Fifteen minutes later she was back at Hideaway Haven.

Joe was the first one she saw when she reached the wide clearing.

"I brought back your bandanna," she told him. "And look at these!" She showed him the flowers.

"Those flowers are wild orchids," Joe told her.

"They're gorgeous!" Michelle said. "And

thanks for showing me that secret path. I've never seen anything like it!"

Joe grinned at her. "It is pretty nice," he agreed.

"The best part was the swimming hole," Michelle went on.

Joe's smile suddenly faded. "What swimming hole?"

"You mean you don't know?" Michelle's mouth dropped open. "Wow! I can't believe it. I found a secret swimming hole. It was fantastic! It was this emerald-green pool—right off the path you showed me—"

"Michelle, you didn't go in, did you?" Joe cut her off.

"Sure I did. I had a great swim and—"

Joe started pacing back and forth. "This is awful," he muttered. "I mean, seriously, incredibly terrible!"

Michelle felt a pang of alarm. "Why? What did I do wrong?" she asked in a small voice.

"I told you to stay on the path." Joe was almost yelling now. "I didn't tell you to go through the bushes. Especially not to any swimming hole!"

"B-but I didn't hurt anything," Michelle explained. "What's the problem? You said it was perfectly safe around here."

"It *is* safe," Joe replied. "Except for one place."

Joe looked sick. He swallowed hard and his voice dropped to a whisper. "Except for the Green Lagoon."

Michelle felt a shiver of fear. "The Green Lagoon? Is that the place I swam in?"

Joe nodded.

"But it seemed really nice," Michelle protested. She thought of the lovely, warm, sparkling water. It was so peaceful. "What's wrong with it?" she asked him. "It can't be anything serious."

"Oh, it's serious all right," Joe told her. "The Green Lagoon is *cursed!*"

Chapter 5

Stephanie hit the beach and started jogging. *Well, maybe we're not staying at a luxurious resort,* she thought. *But at least I can check out the Hawaiian Hideaway and see what one looks like!*

She ran for a while along the water's edge, enjoying the cool waves washing over her feet. She stopped when she saw the hotel in front of her.

The Hawaiian Hideaway's first building was only one story high. It had whitewashed walls and a thatched roof—just like the huts at Hideaway Haven. The rest of the resort was very different, though.

Stephanie crossed a soft green lawn to the main building. Built of pale pink stone, it was three stories high. Each level was lined with wide balconies. Stephanie couldn't actually see into any of the rooms, but she was sure they were huge and gorgeous.

The best thing about the main building was that it curved around the biggest—and coolest—swimming pool she had ever seen. It had three diving boards and a twisting water slide.

She hurried closer. The pool was connected to a second, lower pool by a wide, curving river. Hotel guests floated down the river on inner tubes, then spun into the lower pool.

Stephanie tried not to gape. It was the most fantastic place she had ever seen.

She wondered what was beyond the second pool. A third? No. She caught her breath in amazement. A waterfall cascaded down a steep rock cliff. And on the side of the waterfall, a stairway of pink stone led down to a private, protected ocean cove.

Stephanie made her way down the stairs. Her eyes darted from the cove's crescent-shaped beach to the sailboats skimming across the blue Pacific beyond it.

Now, this was her idea of the perfect tropical resort! It was just as great as it appeared in her guidebook, she thought. Yup—there were even refreshment stands set up right on the beach.

Stephanie slowed as she passed the nearest stand. The attendant glanced up and caught her eye.

"Care for a cold drink, miss?" he asked in a pleasant voice.

"Oh, no. I'm not, uh—" Stephanie began to say. She meant to explain that she wasn't a guest at the Hawaiian Hideaway.

"You look like you need something special," the young man said before she could go on.

He quickly mixed up something yellow and frothy. He added a cherry and a tiny paper umbrella and handed the drink to her.

"A double coconut-pineapple shake," he explained. "It's my specialty. You can't refuse," he added in a teasing voice.

Stephanie smiled and accepted the drink. She took a polite sip. It was completely delicious! She couldn't help it. She quickly drank it all down.

"See?" The young man smiled happily. "I knew you needed that! I'm Brad, by the way."

"Thanks, Brad." Stephanie set the empty glass on the counter. "That was totally perfect!"

"Try some of the popcorn-fried shrimp," Brad insisted. He slid a plate toward her.

"I guess I can't say no," Stephanie said with a laugh. Then she thanked Brad and climbed the stairs to the pools, clutching her plateful of shrimp.

Wow! How pretty the grounds were. Small gardens surrounded the lower pool. They filled the air with the scent of the bright tropical flowers. Hotel guests floated on pink and orange reclining chairs set right into the water. Everyone here looked totally relaxed—and pampered.

Total luxury! Stephanie thought. *And I'm stuck at Hideaway Haven all week!*

The Haven didn't even have one pool, much less two. And snacks on the beach? Forget it! Not unless you packed your own.

"Watch out!" someone called, and grabbed Stephanie's arm.

Stephanie glanced up in surprise. A tall, dark-haired, dark-eyed boy smiled down at her.

"You almost stepped on those sunglasses," he said. He bent down and scooped up the sunglasses. "I'm Lonnie," he introduced himself. "The lifeguard on duty."

"I'm Stephanie. And, uh, I guess you just saved the life of those sunglasses," she joked.

I can't believe I said that! Stephanie felt her cheeks flame in embarrassment. *How nerdy.*

Lonnie laughed. "No kidding—it's the most lifeguard action I had all day," he said.

Stephanie stared at him. He had a terrific laugh. Warm and friendly.

"Sometimes I work harder as the activities assistant than as the lifeguard," Lonnie went on. "Did you just arrive at the Hawaiian Hideaway?"

"Uh—I guess you could say that," Stephanie answered.

"Well, I hope you're staying long enough," Lonnie told her.

"Long enough for what?" Stephanie asked.

"Long enough for me to see you again." Lonnie grinned, showing off his incredible dimples.

Stephanie grinned back at him. She couldn't believe it. Lonnie was really cute, and he was actually flirting with her!

"Hey! Stephanie! Stephanie Tanner, is that you?"

Stephanie glanced up at a pretty girl with a single light-brown braid tossed over one shoulder.

"Amber?" Stephanie gasped.

Amber Michaels smiled back at her.

"Wow. This is totally incredible. Amber goes to my school, back in San Francisco," Stephanie explained to Lonnie.

Stephanie liked Amber, although they weren't close friends. They each hung around with their own crowd back at John Muir Middle School.

Stephanie had always wanted to get to know Amber better. Now it was definitely nice to see a familiar face so far from home.

"I didn't know you were coming here for vacation," Amber said.

"I didn't know *you* were in Hawaii, either," Stephanie replied.

"Yup. This is a great hotel, isn't it?" Amber asked.

"It seems fantastic," Stephanie agreed. "I mean, that water slide looks incredible."

"Haven't you tried it yet?" Amber asked.

"Me? Uh—no, not yet." Stephanie saw Amber glance at the plateful of shrimp in her hand. *She thinks I'm a guest here!* Stephanie suddenly realized. "Oh! You see, I'm not a—"

"Amber was the first one on the slide yesterday," Lonnie cut in before Stephanie could finish.

"How did you remember that?" Amber asked him.

"Because you were also the first one to come to the activities desk and sign up for hula lessons," Lonnie told her.

"Hula lessons?" Stephanie echoed. She remembered how graceful and lovely the hula dancers at the airport had looked. "That sounds like fun."

"We'll see," Amber said. She rolled her eyes. "I'm not exactly known for being the world's best dancer. But the hula looked so cool, I just had to try it."

"You'll do great," Lonnie assured her. "Mahina, our teacher, is a native Hawaiian. I've seen her teach eighty-six-year-old grandmothers the traditional hula dances. *Everyone* looks good when they work with Mahina."

Stephanie felt a pang of envy. Hula classes were exactly the kind of thing she was hoping to have this week. And there were certainly no hula lessons at the Haven!

Amber adjusted the beaded bracelet that she wore around her wrist. "Well, the first lesson is *supposed* to be this afternoon. But we still need one more person to sign up for the class before it's definite."

"We?" Stephanie asked.

"I met some really nice girls here at the Hideaway," Amber explained. "We all agreed to sign up together. But we need one more person to have enough for a class. The hotel has a five-person minimum."

Lonnie tugged gently on a loose strand of Stephanie's blond hair. "I bet Stephanie is the person you've been waiting for," he said. His dark eyes met hers. "How about signing up?"

"Me?" Stephanie asked. "No! I mean—I can't take hula lessons. I'm not—"

"No excuses," Lonnie interrupted her with a grin. "I'd be ducking my duty as activities coordinator if I let you get away with not signing up. The classes are free, and you look like you'd be a terrific dancer."

Stephanie tried to explain. "It's just that I can't because—"

"Hey, Amber! Heard anything about our lessons yet?" Three girls about Stephanie's age walked up to them.

Two of the girls wore bathing suits with tank dresses pulled over them. One had short blond hair. The other had tightly braided black hair. The third and tallest girl wore a cropped red T-shirt, black cotton sweats, and a red hibiscus pinned in her straight black hair.

"Stephanie, meet Laura, and Patricia, and Molly," Amber introduced her friends. "They're the other girls in the hula class." She turned to her friends. "Sorry, guys. We haven't got enough people signed up yet."

Molly, the tall girl, sighed in disappointment.

"Don't give up," Lonnie told her. "All you have to do is convince Stephanie to join your group, and you're rockin'."

Molly's eyes widened with excitement. "Oh, you have just *got* to sign up," she told Stephanie. "I've been wanting to learn hula dancing since I saw it on TV when I was four. But I live in Montana, which is total snow country. So now that I'm finally in Hawaii, I can't blow my big chance. You've got to help us!"

Patricia laughed. "We *all* really want to take hula lessons."

"Not that we're pressuring you to sign up or anything." Laura laughed.

Stephanie laughed with her. She already liked Amber's new friends.

"Don't forget the best part," Patricia added. "The luau."

"That's a big feast the hotel is having on Friday night," Lonnie explained. "Sort of like a giant party on the beach. Everyone who takes hula classes gets to perform there. And Mahina always plans something special for the luau."

"That sounds great," Stephanie admitted.

"Come on," Patricia urged. "The lessons are free. And it's a great chance to learn about Hawaii and have fun! Is there any reason *not* to sign up?"

Actually, I feel exactly the same way, Stephanie thought.

She really wanted those lessons. Learning the hula would be so cool. And if she didn't sign up, there wouldn't be any classes at all— for anyone!

Molly would have to go back to Montana hula-less!

Taking the lessons would be doing a favor for Amber and all her new friends, Stephanie reasoned.

Also, taking the lessons would help her enjoy her vacation. And that's what her dad said he wanted for her.

So what if she wasn't actually a guest of the Hawaiian Hideaway? By taking the lessons, Stephanie wouldn't be harming anyone or anything.

"Okay," Stephanie finally decided. "Sign me up. Hawaiian hula, here I come!"

Chapter 6

Cursed?" Michelle stared at Joe in disbelief. "What do you mean, the Green Lagoon is cursed?"

"Shhh!" Joe grabbed Michelle's arm. He pulled her away from the clearing to a spot where no one would hear them.

"You shouldn't have gone anywhere near the Green Lagoon," he whispered. "An evil spirit lives there, in the water. It doesn't like to be disturbed."

"You're kidding, right?" Michelle asked.

"I wish," Joe answered in a shaky voice.

Michelle didn't believe in curses, but the

45

fact that Joe sounded so scared did make her a little uneasy.

Then she remembered something Danny told her when she was four and was sure they had a ghost in the bathroom. *"Sometimes things are scary because you don't understand them. So if something scares you, try to find out what's really going on."*

When Michelle found out what was really going on in the bathroom, she discovered that the "ghost" was really just a rattling pipe.

"Okay." Michelle folded her arms. "So what's supposed to happen if you disturb the spirit?"

"I don't know what will happen." Joe sounded miserable. "Except that the spirit will get really angry."

"And what exactly does that mean?" Michelle asked.

Joe shook his head. "Well, according to the legend, when the spirit gets mad, the one who bothered it is showered with bad luck."

"Like . . . what kind of bad luck?"

"I'm not sure," Joe said. "No one's ever disturbed the spirit before. Not while I've lived here, anyway."

"Then how do you even know there really *is* a curse?" Michelle argued.

"This guy stayed here about two weeks ago," Joe explained. "He said that the people who lived around here a long time ago believed that anyone who swam in the Green Lagoon would be cursed."

Michelle rolled her eyes. "And you *believe* that guy? He probably just liked making up stories to scare you."

"I don't think so," Joe said in a grim tone. "This guy's a scientist. An archaeologist."

"Oh." Michelle knew that archaeologists didn't make up stuff like that. Still, she needed to get all the facts. "So, do you know where I can find this archaeologist?" she asked. "I think I'd better ask him some questions."

"He went off somewhere on the island to dig up old bones or something. I haven't seen him again." Joe looked worried. "I just hope you're going to be okay."

Michelle spread her arms. "Look, I'm fine. Really."

Joe shook his head. "Not the way this guy told it. He said from the moment you swim in the lagoon the bad luck stays with you. And it gets stronger and stronger—until the night of the full moon."

"Then the bad luck stops, right?" Michelle said.

Joe looked her straight in the eye. "No. Then something *really* terrible happens."

Michelle couldn't help it. A shiver ran down her spine. "What kind of something?"

"I don't know," Joe admitted.

"That's it!" Michelle snapped. "I've had it with this dumb story. We're both forgetting one very important thing."

"What?" Joe looked suspicious.

"There's no such thing as evil spirits. Or curses," Michelle declared. She folded her arms across her chest.

This time Joe was the one who rolled his eyes. "Of course there are."

"Listen." Michelle tried to sound reasonable. "No matter what some archaeologist says, I don't believe in any of that stuff. Just like I don't believe in ghosts or monsters. There's no curse on me. Period."

She started back along the path that circled

behind the huts. "Now, come on. I want to find my dad and—"

Michelle's speech broke off as the tip of her sandal caught in a tree root. She stumbled and threw out her arms to steady herself. But she couldn't keep from falling.

Snap!

The sandal strap broke in half, and Michelle landed hard on the ground.

"Are you okay?" Joe leaned over and held out a hand to help her up.

"Yeah." Michelle rubbed her knees. They were covered with dirt.

"Rats," she said, glancing down at her ruined sandal. "I can't believe it! The strap broke right in half. And these sandals are brand new!"

Joe's eyes grew wide. He backed away from her.

"What's wrong?" Michelle asked.

"Bad luck!" Joe shouted. "The curse. Don't you see? It's already starting!"

"Don't be silly," Michelle told him. "Anyone could break a sandal strap. It doesn't mean I'm cursed."

Becky appeared in the clearing. "Michelle!"

49

she called. "Want to come to the beach? Jesse made sandwiches and lemonade in the Haven's kitchen. There's enough for all of us."

"Great," Michelle called back. She turned to Joe. "See?" she said. "I'm going on a picnic at the beach. Does that sound like bad luck to you?"

Michelle hurried down to the beach. She smiled as she heard Joe's footsteps behind her. She couldn't be in too much trouble if Joe was willing to tag along. If things were really as scary as he had said, he would be staying as far away from her as possible.

She found Jesse, Becky, and the twins spread out on a plaid beach blanket. Jesse was covering the twins with baby sunblock. When he was done, he handed the tube to Michelle. "Here, kiddo. You don't want to burn."

Michelle slathered the sunblock on.

"Okay, now it's time to eat," Becky declared. "All set for your first feast in paradise?"

"Totally," Michelle answered. "I am so hungry."

"You're welcome to eat with us, too, Joe," Becky said.

"Thanks." Joe knelt down beside Alex and helped him fill his pail with sand.

"So where's the food?" Michelle called out over the sound of the waves.

Jesse pointed to a large flat boulder that stuck up from the sand. A large blue and white plastic cooler sat on top of it.

"We've got tuna fish, peanut butter and jelly, egg salad, and cream cheese and olives," Jesse told them. "What do you want?"

"Definitely not the olive kind," Michelle said. "I'll have tuna fish."

"Peanut butter for me," Joe said.

"And me!" Nicky chimed in.

"I want lemonade," Alex said.

"That's not a sandwich." Jesse laughed and stood up and started toward the cooler.

"Oh, look!" Becky shielded her eyes with one hand and pointed to the sky. Three large, long-necked birds flew over the beach. "Those look almost like Canada geese," she said.

"They can't be." Uncle Jesse studied the sky, too. "According to the nature guide I read, you don't see Canada geese in this part of the Pacific."

"They're called *Nene*. They're native Hawaiian geese and our state bird," Joe explained. Michelle watched the birds skim the top of a large wave as it crashed into the shore.

"You almost never see Nene on this part of the island," Joe remarked.

Aunt Becky smiled at him. "Wow. Then we're really lucky we saw them."

Michelle gave Joe a gentle poke. "So much for bad luck!" she whispered.

"Hey!" Jesse said suddenly. "What happened to our cooler?" He pointed to the flat rock. "I set it right there. And now it's gone!"

"Maybe the geese took it," Nicky said.

"I don't think so." Jesse scratched his head.

"Look!" Michelle pointed out to the Pacific. There was a blue and white shape bobbing way out in the water. "Our lunch got swept away by a wave."

"Go get it!" Alex said.

"I can't," Uncle Jesse told him. He looked upset. "It's already too far out."

Problems in Paradise

Uncle Jesse gave Joe and Michelle an apologetic look. "Sorry, you guys. I guess I'll have to go make more sandwiches before anyone can eat. I should have noticed that the tide was coming in."

Joe poked Michelle in the ribs. "You see?" he whispered. "I was right. The curse *is* working!"

Michelle shook her head. "No way," she argued. "The curse didn't sweep our lunch out to sea. You heard Uncle Jesse. He just didn't notice that the tide was coming in."

"That wasn't just the tide. It was the curse," Joe insisted. "The Curse of the Green Lagoon made the cooler disappear!"

Chapter
7

Don't swim out too far," Danny warned Stephanie.

"Don't worry, Dad. I'll just be out beyond those rocks." Stephanie pointed to where the beach curved around a row of big rocks. It was their second day in Hawaii but Stephanie's first attempt at snorkeling on the island. She hoped it wouldn't make her dad too nervous.

Danny gave her an easy smile. "Okay. Have fun!" he said. He pulled his hat over his eyes and settled down for a nap.

Stephanie stared at him in disbelief. *Is that really my father?* she wondered. *He's so relaxed!*

Problems in Paradise

Danny Tanner believed in being prepared. Back home, he would have given her a detailed list of dangers to avoid while she was snorkeling. Here in Hawaii, he seemed confident that Stephanie would be careful. Weird.

Stephanie pulled the snorkel mask over her head. She placed the breathing tube in her mouth and waded into the surf.

Wow! The waters off Maui were home to zillions of colorful, amazing fish! Blue, yellow, red fish—they flitted this way and that in front of her eyes. She felt as if she could swim for hours, admiring them.

Of course, I'd really rather be taking my second hula lesson right now, she thought.

Her lesson the day before was great. Their teacher, Mahina, was terrific. She smiled as she remembered the end of class when Mahina said she was "a natural." Also, it was fun to hang out with Amber and her friends.

Stephanie had already told Amber that her family might be leaving Hawaii today, so she wouldn't be able to make it to the next class.

I am not going back there again, she decided.

After all, I took that class only to help out Amber and her friends. Those lessons are really for guests of the Hawaiian Hideaway. Not the guests of Hideaway Haven!

Suddenly Stephanie saw something green moving in the sand on the ocean floor. She swam a little lower to get a better look.

Wow! It was a green sea turtle—a baby one!

Intrigued, Stephanie followed it, swimming right alongside it until it dove down to the floor of the ocean again. It disappeared in a swirl of sand.

Whew! Stephanie swam for the shore. She was totally getting tired. It was time to take a break.

She rode a wave into the beach. Then she pulled off her snorkel mask and shook out the water that had collected inside. The sun began drying her off immediately.

"Hey, Stephanie!" a voice called out.

Stephanie turned. It was Amber!

"What are you doing here?" she asked, her friend surprised.

Amber waded out of the water. "Same as you. Swimming."

Stephanie looked around. Whoops! She had swum a lot farther than she realized. Almost directly up to the shore at the Hawaiian Hideaway Hotel!

"Did your dad change his mind?" Amber asked. She sounded excited.

"My dad?"

"Didn't you say you couldn't come to today's hula lesson because your dad might cut his vacation short?" Amber questioned.

"Oh. Right. My dad. What happened was"—Stephanie thought fast—"we were all packed and ready to go to the airport. Then he got this call from San Francisco. We didn't have to fly back today after all."

"That's fantastic!" Amber said. "That means we can still have hula classes! We still have the right number of participants."

Stephanie shut her eyes. How did she get herself into these situations? She wished she could just disappear in a swirl of sand like the little sea turtle.

"Uh—I'm not sure I want to take class today," Stephanie told Amber. "I'm not very good at it. And—"

"But we need you," Amber insisted. "We can't have the class without five people."

Stephanie's stomach felt tied up in knots. She'd been so positive about not going back to the Hawaiian Hideaway. About not having to pretend that she was a guest there. But now she felt cornered. Trapped.

Amber glanced at her waterproof watch. "If we go back to the hotel right now, we can still make the class. Come on!" She grabbed her towel and started down the beach toward the resort.

Stephanie stood perfectly still. This was it. She should be honest with Amber now. She should just tell her that she'd never been a guest at the Hawaiian Hideaway. That she didn't belong at the hula lessons in the first place.

Stephanie took a shaky breath. How bad could Amber's reaction be? After all, it was the truth.

"Stephanie, come on!" Amber shouted. "Molly and the others are going to be so glad to see you! Now we can all be part of the luau!"

Stephanie felt totally trapped. She didn't

want to go back to the Hideaway, but if she didn't, four other people would miss a chance to do something that really mattered to them.

It was settled. She *had* to take the class.

Molly, Laura, and Patricia were already waiting at the dance pavilion, a covered platform set up halfway between the lower pool and the beach. A thatched roof kept it shady. The open sides let the ocean breezes blow through.

"You're back!" Patricia cried.

"I thought my hula-dancing days were over," Molly joked.

Stephanie glanced from one girl to another. They all seemed so happy that she was back. How could she even consider letting them down?

Lonnie came over while they waited for Mahina to show up.

"You guys looked great yesterday," he told them. He turned to Stephanie. "I'm on lifeguard duty now at the pool. But maybe I'll see you around after your class?"

"Um, I don't know. Maybe," Stephanie replied with a shrug.

"Great." Lonnie grinned, flashing those amazing dimples before he strode away.

"Wow. I think he really likes you," Amber said.

Patricia poked Stephanie in the side. "He definitely likes you."

Stephanie flushed. "He *is* really nice, isn't he?"

"Hey, girls! Ready for our second class?" a voice spoke up. Mahina stood at the edge of the stage. She was holding an armful of grass skirts. "One for each of you, because you're such a great class!" she explained. She gave them all a wide, warm smile.

Mahina was young and pretty, with beautiful long black hair and sparkling eyes. "Take a skirt and slip it on," she said. "It will make a real difference in your dancing."

Stephanie put on a skirt and swung her hips. The grass made a soft rustling sound. She felt like a real hula dancer.

"Okay, yesterday I told you a bit about how hula dancing began," Mahina said. "If you lived in old Hawaii, you girls would be called *Olapa*. That means you are a group of young, agile dancers. The older women would be in a separate group. They would do the chanting while you danced."

Mahina started a cassette tape of music mixed with traditional chants. "There are six basic hula moves. Every hula dance is made up of combinations of them, so they are really all you have to know. Let's try our third move today."

Mahina began to dance as she spoke. Her hips and arms swayed gently. "All hula movements imitate nature," she went on. "For instance, the movements of fluttering leaves or birds in flight."

When Mahina danced, Stephanie felt as if she really could see leaves falling from a tree and birds taking to the air. Mahina danced as if she were a part of the island itself.

"Okay, girls. Now you try it. Start with your hips," Mahina instructed. "Try to sway from the waist down. And try not to move your rib cage."

Stephanie found that part more difficult than it sounded. When she moved her hips, her rib cage definitely wanted to move the same way.

"All your movements should be very soft," Mahina explained to them. She gently adjusted Patricia's arm so that she held it properly.

"Wow! That looks much better," Laura told her.

Mahina moved among the girls, correcting their positions.

"Is this right?" Stephanie raised her arms overhead, then lowered them.

"Lovely," Mahina said. "Your movements really flow. As I said yesterday, you're a natural."

Stephanie felt herself blushing at the praise.

Mahina showed them two more moves. Then they combined all of the moves they'd learned into different steps.

Stephanie had to concentrate hard, but it was fun. She loved the music and the flowing movements. She was having such a good time that she was surprised when Mahina smiled and said, "Okay. That's our lesson for today."

Patricia seemed disappointed. "Do we have to give the skirts back?" she asked.

"I'm afraid so," Mahina said. "But I promise

to bring them back. Good work, girls. See you at our next lesson!"

"You will," Laura promised. "No question."

But Stephanie had a few questions. The main one was: How long could she continue to take classes before someone found out that she wasn't actually staying at the Hawaiian Hideaway Hotel?

Then there was the question of her family. How long till Danny discovered what was going on? What would she do then?

There has to be a way I can make this all work out, she told herself.

"Hey, Stephanie," Amber said. "Let's grab some drinks at the snack bar."

Stephanie hesitated. She was definitely thirsty after the hula class and her swim. A cold drink sounded great, but she knew it wasn't a good idea to hang out at the hotel.

"Um . . . thanks, but I shouldn't," she said.

"Why not?" Molly wanted to know.

Stephanie got to her feet. Her mind raced. *I could say I have to baby-sit for my little cousins,* she reasoned. *Except a ritzy hotel like this would have plenty of on-staff baby-sitters. Maybe I could tell them . . .*

Patricia glanced at her watch. Her eyebrows rose. "Whoa! I said I'd meet my mom for a hike in fifteen minutes. So we'll make it a fast drink, okay?"

Fifteen minutes, Stephanie thought. *That's no big deal.*

She followed Amber and the others to the refreshment stand. The attendant whipped up a batch of pineapple smoothies.

This is nuts, she thought, waiting for her drink. *I can't keep up this act of being a Hawaiian Hideaway guest. It feels wrong—and it's making me completely paranoid. I feel like someone's going to catch me at any moment.*

I just have to be honest and tell them, Stephanie decided. *Before someone discovers that I don't belong here.*

"Guys," Stephanie started. She stood up to make her announcement.

"Miss Tanner!" a voice exclaimed. "Stop right there."

"Yikes!" Stephanie nearly leaped off her chair. Too late—she was busted! She was going to look like a total loser in front of Amber and her friends!

Stephanie glanced up and found Mahina smiling down at her. *Whew!* Stephanie breathed a sigh of relief. Just Mahina.

"Sorry I startled you," Mahina said. "Can I ask you a question?"

"Sure." Stephanie's heart pounded.

"As you know, the hula class is performing at the luau this Friday," Mahina began. "I was wondering if you would mind being the lead dancer in our performance."

Stephanie's jaw dropped open. "Are you kidding?" she finally asked. "You want me to be the lead?"

"Will you do it?" Mahina asked Stephanie. "It means you'll have to work a little harder than the others."

"I—I guess so," Stephanie said, stunned.

"Great!" Mahina smiled broadly. "See you in class tomorrow." She walked off toward the beach.

"Stephanie, this is so fantastic!" Laura squealed.

"What's fantastic?" asked an amused voice.

Stephanie looked up and felt her cheeks blushing again. Lonnie was smiling down at her. Oh, he was soooo cute!

"Mahina just asked Stephanie to be the lead dancer for our class at the luau performance," Molly replied.

"Wow, you must be good!" Lonnie acted impressed. "I can't wait to see you at the show."

"Me, either," Amber said. Then she added in a whisper, "Your dad really can't cut short your vacation now, Steph. You've just got to dance at the luau. We are totally psyched for you. And so is Lonnie!"

Amber was right, Stephanie realized. Hula dancing at the luau was an amazing opportunity. She'd be absolutely crazy to throw it away.

Wouldn't she?

MICHELLE

Chapter
8

Michelle sat in her living room back home in San Francisco. Her golden retriever, Comet, was jumping all over her, trying to lick her face.

"Down, boy," Michelle told him. "Cut it out!"

Comet kept jumping up on her anyway. Each time he jumped, his claws scratched her lightly. Making her itch. Soon she was itching all over.

"Michelle, wake up!" Comet called.

That's weird, Michelle thought. *Comet can talk! And he sounds like . . . Stephanie?*

*   *   *

"Michelle! Wake up!"

Michelle opened her eyes. She wasn't back in San Francisco. She was in her bed in Hideaway Haven. Morning light was streaming into the hut, and Stephanie was shaking her by the shoulder.

Michelle sat up in bed and scratched her shoulder.

"What's wrong with you?" Stephanie asked. "You were tossing and—"

Stephanie suddenly stopped talking. She peered closely at Michelle. A funny look came over her face. "What is *that?*"

"What's what?" Michelle asked, alarmed. She scratched her left arm. Then her right arm. Then her neck. She glanced down.

"Yikes!" she cried. Her whole body was covered with little red bumps, and they all itched like crazy!

"It's like my dream, only worse!" She lifted her pajama top. Oh, no! There were bumps on her stomach, too. *It can't be the chicken pox,* she decided. *I already had the chicken pox.*

"Don't move, Michelle," Stephanie ordered. "I'm getting Dad."

Michelle scratched under her armpits. She scratched the back of her neck. She was scratching her shins when Danny raced into the hut.

"Stay calm, Michelle," he told her. "It looks like a pretty nasty rash to me. Think, sweetheart—did you get any insect bites since we've been here? Or did you walk through a patch of suspicious-looking leaves? Like poison ivy?"

"No," Michelle told him. "I definitely didn't see any poison ivy. I don't remember getting any bug bites."

Danny asked Stephanie to get the anti-itching cream from his first aid kit.

"In the meantime," he told Michelle, "try to think back over everything you did since we got here. For instance, did you eat anything unusual?"

"No," Michelle told him. "Just ordinary stuff. The first day I had a tuna sandwich when I ate on the beach with Becky and Jesse. Yesterday I had cereal, then peanut butter and jelly for lunch, and then that vegetable thing we all had for dinner."

"You couldn't be allergic to any of that," Danny said. "I think I'd better call a doctor. You stay here. I'll be right back."

Stephanie returned with the itch cream. She helped Michelle smooth it over her rash.

"This stuff is goopy," Michelle complained. "Even goopier than the twins' sunblock."

"Well, use plenty of it," Stephanie told her. "You want that rash to calm down so you can come to the beach with us."

"The beach?" Michelle shook her head. "No way. I'm not wearing a bathing suit with these bumps all over my skin. Besides, I've got to stay here until the doctor comes."

Stephanie handed over her portable CD player and a stack of CDs. "You can borrow these. Maybe listening to them will make the time go by more quickly."

"Thanks," Michelle said. But CD player or no CD player, being stuck in the hut was going to totally stink!

She was on her third CD when her father led the doctor into the hut. Dr. Smithe was a round man with a cheery smile.

"So I hear you have a rash," the doctor said. Michelle held out her arm.

"Hmm," he said. He looked at Danny. "She has dermatitis."

70

Michelle gulped. "Is that serious?"

"It just means your skin is irritated," Danny explained.

"Exactly." The doctor nodded. "I don't know what's caused this, but it doesn't look like anything to worry about. I'll give you a cream that should clear it up. And, Michelle, I want you to stay indoors today. Sun could make the rash worse."

Michelle sighed. "But I was going to explore the island some more with Joe today."

"I'm afraid you'll have to change your plans," Danny said.

Michelle sighed. "This is terrible," she muttered. Here she was, on vacation in Hawaii, and she was more bored than she ever was at home! Feeling itchy didn't help, either.

After spending the entire morning in her hut, Michelle knew she had to get out—or she would die of boredom. She hopped off her bed and changed into loose-fitting khaki pants and a long-sleeved shirt. She glanced in the mirror. The clothes hid most of her rash. At least this way she could wander around a bit, and her skin wouldn't be exposed to the sun.

She headed out across the clearing and saw Joe's father talking to the Haven's gardener. The gardener was watering a flower bed with a hose.

"Hi, Mr. Grant," Michelle called.

Mr. Grant turned to her. "Hi, Michelle." He frowned. "How's that rash feeling?"

"It's just—oh, no," Michelle groaned. The gardener had turned to see her rash. Which meant he was no longer looking at the hose. And he was about to spray Mr. Grant with water!

"Watch out!" Michelle yelled. But she was too late.

Water sprayed all over Joe's dad. His hair, face, and shirt were drenched.

The gardener gasped. "Oh, no! Sorry, Mr. Grant!" He quickly aimed the hose in the other direction.

"Are you okay?" Michelle asked Joe's dad. She felt bad. If she hadn't called out to him, the gardener wouldn't have turned to look at her rash.

"I'm fine," Mr. Grant said. Michelle thought he looked really uncomfortable.

"Umm—is Joe around?" Michelle asked.

"He's in the dining hut," Mr. Grant told her.

"Thanks," Michelle called out. She crossed the clearing and entered the large dining hut.

She liked the big, airy room with its long dining table and collection of pottery. Last night, at dinner, she had tried to count all the colorful platters and pitchers stacked in the big, open cupboard at the back of the room. She lost count somewhere around sixty-two.

Now Joe sat on a stepladder in front of the cupboard. He hummed to himself as he put away stacks of freshly washed dishes.

"Hey, Joe," Michelle said.

Joe turned to look at her. His eyes widened. "Whoa! You look terrible!"

"I know," Michelle said. "I woke up with this weird rash all over my body. At least it doesn't itch since Dr. Smithe gave me some cream for it. But no one can figure out where it came from."

"Don't be dumb," Joe told her. "It came from the curse."

"What? No way!" Michelle exclaimed. "People get rashes all the time."

"But you got this rash *after* you got cursed," Joe pointed out.

"This has nothing to do with any curse," Michelle told him. "I told you, there are no such things as curses. And I don't believe in dumb, stupid, evil spirits, either."

"Shhh!" Joe looked frightened. He glanced around the room. "Don't say that. You'll make the spirit even madder."

Fine. I give up, Michelle thought. *If Joe wants to believe in superstitions, that's his problem.*

She decided to change the subject. "Need any help?" she offered.

Joe hesitated. "You mind stacking dishes?"

"Of course not," she said. "I stack dishes at home all the time."

"Great." Joe pointed to the top shelf of the cupboard. A space had been cleared for stacks of dishes. "They go up there. I'll climb up. Then you can hand me the dishes. It won't take long if we work together."

"No problem," Michelle said.

Joe stood up on the stepladder. He turned and held out both hands. "Hand me a few at a time," he said.

"Okay." Michelle took three dishes from the stack on the cupboard's wide bottom shelf.

She handed them to Joe, and he set them neatly on the top shelf.

Michelle handed Joe six more dishes. He put them on the highest shelf in the cupboard.

Crrrreeeeak!

Michelle froze. She glanced up at Joe. "Did you hear that?"

"Yeah." He sounded nervous. "What was it?"

"I don't know," Michelle answered. "It sounds like—"

"Watch out!" Joe yelled.

Michelle leaped back. The entire cupboard wobbled. Then the top shelf collapsed.

Craaash!

Plates flew everywhere.

"Whoa!" Joe exclaimed, leaping sideways.

"Oh, no!" Michelle cried. She covered her face and head with her arms.

Michelle dropped her arms. She and Joe stood surrounded by pieces of broken pottery.

A second later Joe's dad rushed into the room. He gazed at the mess in surprise. "Are you kids okay?" he finally asked.

"Yeah. We're fine," Joe told him.

Michelle stared at the shattered dishes that

covered the floor. She felt her face burning an even brighter red under her rash.

"I'm so sorry, Mr. Grant!" she wailed. "I don't know how it happened."

Mr. Grant stepped over the broken dishes and peered closely at the cupboard. "Looks like the top shelf just gave out," he said. "You know, it's a really old piece of furniture. I guess we just had too much weight on that shelf."

Joe frowned. "Dad—why are you soaking wet?" he asked.

Mr. Grant glanced at his soggy shirt. "Just a silly accident, right, Michelle?" He winked at her. "I guess this is a day for accidents."

Michelle smiled weakly.

"I'll have this mess cleaned up. You kids go have some fun for a little while," Mr. Grant instructed.

Michelle followed Joe out of the dining hut.

"Two accidents in one day?" Joe asked. He stared at her—hard. "And they both happened when you were around?"

"Listen, I know what you're about to say, and those dishes did not break because of any curse," Michelle insisted.

She headed back toward her hut. It was windier now, she noticed. Maybe she'd go down to the beach and see if there were any sailboarders to watch.

Michelle passed a small hut on the side of the trail. Yesterday Joe told her that hut was the oldest one at the Haven. It didn't even have white stucco walls. It was made entirely of grass and wooden poles.

Michelle blinked. Maybe it was her imagination—but she thought she saw the old hut move a little. She stared at it.

And saw the entire grass hut swaying in the wind!

She tried to cry out. But the words froze in her throat.

"The hut!" Joe yelled behind her.

The hut began to topple forward—right onto Michelle!

"Michelle, move!" Joe screamed.

At the last moment, Michelle jumped out of the way. The hut crashed down beside her. Michelle stared at the pile of dried-out grass and wood. This was unbelievable. If she hadn't moved right then, she would have been squashed!

Joe glared at her. "Do you really believe that was an accident, too?" he demanded.

Michelle thought about everything that had happened since she swam in the Green Lagoon. First she had broken her sandal strap. That wasn't so terrible. Then the cooler floated out to sea. Annoying, but no big deal. Then she got her rash. That was pretty awful.

Then the gardener soaked Mr. Grant. Not *too* major. But ten minutes later the top shelf of the cupboard collapsed and all those dishes broke. Now a hut had fallen over—and nearly killed her! Things were getting worse and worse!

Michelle felt her heart sink. What Joe said was true. *All those accidents happened when she was around.*

This was more than bad luck, she realized.

Inside, Michelle knew that there was only one horrible way to explain everything that had happened.

I really am cursed! she realized. *I'm doomed!*

STEPHANIE

Chapter 9

Stephanie glanced at her watch. She had just enough time to get to the Hawaiian Hideaway for her third hula lesson.

It was tough getting away. Her dad wanted her to go for a nature walk with him. Then Michelle had woken up with that rash, and Danny needed to talk with the doctor. So Stephanie told her dad that she was going on a nature walk of her own.

Stephanie felt bad for Michelle. What a bummer to wake up in Hawaii covered in gross red bumps!

Still, Stephanie was relieved that she didn't

have to tell her dad where she was going. Danny loved the Haven. He already felt loyal to it. He wouldn't understand why she wanted to spend so much time over at the Hawaiian Hideaway.

Plus he might think she was being dishonest by taking the lessons. Even though she really wasn't.

Stephanie raced along the hard-packed sand by the water's edge. The wind blew her long blond hair behind her. The ocean's cool spray glistened on her skin. High above her, a pair of birds soared over the waves. She took a deep breath and pushed herself to go faster. Running on the beach was the best!

She glanced at her watch again as the Hawaiian Hideaway's pink walls came into view. *Oh, no!* she thought. *I'm going to be late! Unless . . .*

Stephanie realized that if she cut through the main building of the hotel instead of going around the edge of the beach, she could get to the dance pavilion more quickly.

The idea of actually going into the hotel

made her a little nervous. What if someone recognized her as a non-guest?

I'm being paranoid again, Stephanie quickly decided. *After all, I'm only taking a little short-cut.* She ran straight up to the main building.

She opened the front door and stepped into the lobby. The sound of rushing water greeted her. To the side of the registration desk, a waterfall tumbled over shiny black stones into a swirling pool.

This place is heaven! Stephanie thought. She glanced around. Right behind the waterfall should be a door that would lead back outside—her shortcut to the dance pavilion.

She crossed the lobby and circled the waterfall—but found only huge windows. No door at all.

So much for that idea! Stephanie thought. She checked her watch again. Hula class started in exactly three minutes!

"Excuse me, miss?"

Stephanie turned around slowly.

A woman in an elegant white linen suit smiled at her. She wore a gold tag on her lapel that said MANAGER.

Stephanie gulped hard. The manager! She was caught.

"You look a little lost," the woman said in a kind voice. "Can I help you find something?"

"Um," Stephanie said, "yes. I'm trying to get outside. To the dance pavilion."

"The quickest way is down that hallway," the woman told her. "The hallway curves around to the right. Just follow it to the end, and you'll see a door that leads outside. Then you'll be about twenty yards from the dance pavilion."

"Thank you!" Stephanie said. She walked calmly across the lobby. Then she sprinted down the hall, around the curve—and straight into a young chambermaid wearing the pale pink hotel uniform.

"Ooof!" the chambermaid exclaimed. The huge pile of towels she carried went flying everywhere.

"Oh, no!" Stephanie exclaimed. "I'm so sorry. I can't believe I'm such a klutz!"

"That's all right," the girl said. She kneeled down and began picking up towels.

"I'll help." Stephanie scrambled to grab a handful of towels.

"Thanks," the girl said. "Just stack them up again." She held out her arms.

"No, let me help you. Really. I'll take these," Stephanie offered.

"Thanks. That's really nice of you." The girl backed up toward one of the guest rooms. She fumbled with a set of keys, then finally twisted the lock open.

"I'm bringing them right in here," the girl said.

Stephanie followed her into a huge living room. The couch and chairs were covered in pale lavenders and greens. The colors reminded Stephanie of a calm summer day. A flowering vine framed glass doors that opened onto a tiled terrace.

"Wow. This room is gorgeous!" Stephanie said.

"It's one of the nicest suites in the hotel," the girl agreed.

Stephanie couldn't help feeling curious. "Would it be okay if I stepped out onto the terrace?" she asked the chambermaid.

The girl smiled. "Sure, but not for too long."

Stephanie stepped out onto the terrace's

tiled floor. In the distance she saw the sparkling blue ocean cove.

Then she heard someone call her name. Surprised, she turned to her right. Amber and Molly were waving frantically from the lawn in front of the dance pavilion. "Come on," Amber called. "You're going to be late for class!"

"Be right there!" Stephanie called back. "I'd better go," she told the chambermaid. "But thanks."

"No problem," the girl replied.

Stephanie crossed the living room and ran down the hallway and outside. She raced across the lawn. She didn't see Mahina, but Amber and the other girls were already waiting in the dance pavilion.

Stephanie jogged over to them. "Sorry I'm late," she called.

Amber grinned at her. "I'm just glad I spotted you out on your balcony."

"Yeah, your room must have an incredible view," Molly added.

"Huh?" Stephanie said.

"Yeah. You're staying in one of the nicest

places in the resort," Amber agreed. "I mean, my room has a nice view. But I bet it's nothing like yours."

"Uh, I—" Stephanie stuttered. Did they all think she was staying in the most expensive part of the Hawaiian Hideaway resort?

"Listen, it's not like that at all," Stephanie protested. This was getting out of hand, she realized. Now she would *have* to admit she was staying at the Haven.

"Listen. Really, my room isn't all that—" she began.

"I'm sorry," Amber cut her off. "I didn't mean to sound like I was jealous of your suite or anything."

"No, no, you didn't say anything wrong," Stephanie assured her. "It's just that I'm not—"

"Aloha, everyone!" Mahina rushed up onto the stage. She was carrying an armful of grass skirts. "I'm sorry I'm so late. My last class—at the senior center—got a little carried away." She laughed. "The older folks just didn't want to stop dancing!"

She handed out the skirts, then slipped a tape in the cassette player. The sounds of a

Hawaiian guitar and a rhythmic drum filled the pavilion.

"Let's start with what we practiced yesterday," Mahina said. "Then I'll teach you the dance that our class will be performing on Friday night."

Stephanie tried to concentrate on her hula dancing, but her mind kept wandering to her hotel room situation. She had to tell the others the truth. Especially Amber, if she wanted to stay friends with her when they got back to San Francisco.

You can't be a real friend and lie, Stephanie thought.

"Stephanie, where are you?" Mahina asked. "Somehow I don't think you're with the rest of us."

Stephanie suddenly realized that everyone else was facing the ocean—and she was facing the hotel! She turned around quickly. "Sorry," she murmured. She felt completely flustered.

"Are you all right?" Mahina asked.

"Fine. I—I just got a little distracted," Stephanie explained.

The dance teacher smiled. "Well, try to concentrate from now on. You've got a lot to learn before the luau on Friday."

"I know." Stephanie tried to smile back. *Will Amber and the other girls even be talking to me on Friday?* she wondered.

"Small step to the right," Mahina called out. "And step and step and *turn!*"

For the rest of the class Stephanie focused on hula dancing. The class helped calm her fears—a little.

"All right, dancers. This will be the last combination for today," Mahina finally announced.

When the class ended and Stephanie began to slip off her grass skirt, Mahina stopped her.

"Not you, Stephanie," the dance teacher said. "I need you to stay a little longer. I want to show you the solo dance you'll be doing on Friday night."

Stephanie didn't know whether she should be disappointed or relieved. She really needed to make this confession. At the same time, it was kind of nice to know that she wasn't going to be totally humiliated in the next two minutes.

Mahina changed the tape in the boom box. "At the luau, after our class performs, I'm going to clap my hands once. Then the rest of the class will step back. And you'll step forward for your solo."

Mahina demonstrated a short, graceful dance.

"I think I recognize some of those steps," Stephanie said.

"You do," Mahina assured her. "It's just a new combination of the movements you've already learned. The hardest thing will be not getting the two patterns mixed up. Why don't you walk through it with me?"

Twenty minutes later Mahina snapped off the tape. "Good work," she told Stephanie. "You're going to do fine."

She took a deep breath, waved good-bye to Mahina, and headed toward the pool. She was pretty sure she'd find the other girls there. *Okay, here goes*, she thought. *I'm going to come clean. My time as a "guest of the Hawaiian Hideaway" is officially over.*

Her heart sank as she realized she might have just had her last hula lesson. She hated to disappoint Mahina. Especially now that she'd learned her dance. But she had a feeling that once she confessed, she'd never be able to go near the resort again. She'd be way too embarrassed to face Amber and the others.

But I can't go on feeling this way, she reminded herself. It was as if someone might come up to her at any minute and yell out the truth: Stephanie Tanner doesn't belong here!

Stephanie reached the lower pool. She didn't see the girls anywhere, so she headed for the stairs that led to the beach. It was weird. She'd spent so much time at the Hideaway, she knew her way around. It almost felt as if she were staying there. *Almost.*

"Stephanie!" Lonnie waved to her from the lifeguard stand on the edge of the pool. "Wait up a minute, would you?"

Stephanie waited while he said something to the lifeguard beside him. Then he climbed down the high ladder and jogged over to her.

"Hey." He gave her his warm grin—the one that made her heart speed up. "What's up?"

I'm about to tell everyone what a fake I am, Stephanie thought. She ignored her racing heart. After all, it wasn't as if she were going to be seeing Lonnie again.

"I'm looking for Amber and the others," she answered in a casual tone. "Have you seen them?"

Lonnie shook his head. "No, I've been concentrating on the shallow end of the pool. I had to break up a major chicken fight earlier."

"Well, I guess I'll look for them down by the cove," Stephanie said.

She started toward the staircase. Then she felt Lonnie touch her arm lightly. She turned around, surprised.

"Listen," he said. "After the luau on Friday night, want to go for a walk on the beach? There's going to be a full moon. The ocean's really amazing then—it goes all silver in the moonlight."

Stephanie stared at Lonnie. A walk on the beach under a full moon? It was totally the most romantic thing she could think of.

There was only one problem with the plan. She wasn't going to the luau, because as soon as she told everyone the truth, she'd more than likely be a complete outcast.

"You're not answering." Lonnie sounded nervous. "I guess that means you *don't* want to go for a walk with me."

"No, I do!" Stephanie said. "I mean, I would really love to."

"Excellent!" Lonnie smiled.

"Hey, Lonnie, get back here!" the other lifeguard yelled. "You already took your break."

"I've got to run," Lonnie said. He gave her that amazing smile again. "But I'll see you at the luau!" He jogged off.

Stephanie stood there stunned. *How on earth do I get into these situations?* she wondered.

She walked over and scanned the white beach below. Laura and Patricia lay on a striped beach blanket. Amber and Molly bodysurfed along a perfect wave.

Stephanie hesitated. She had planned to tell the girls the truth, but was that really the best idea? Mahina was counting on her doing her solo on Friday night. And now there was something else. Lonnie was counting on a moonlight walk afterward.

Would it be so terrible if I didn't tell everyone

that I'm staying at the Haven? Stephanie asked herself.

After all, she reasoned, *it's not some big, terrible secret. It's not like I robbed a bank or anything.*

Stephanie pictured herself at the luau on Friday night, in the center of the stage. She was wearing a grass skirt, a lei, and flowers in her hair. She was doing the dance she'd just learned. Lonnie and Mahina watched her every move. Then they both applauded like crazy. All the people in the audience were on their feet, clapping! Then it was just Lonnie and Stephanie, walking along a moonlit beach. . . .

No way can I give up hula lessons now! Stephanie decided. *I'm just going to have to find a way around this whole hotel mix-up. Because, no matter what, the show must go on!*

MICHELLE

Chapter 10

Michelle shoved aside a huge pile of books. Then she laid her head down on the table in front of her. "Ugh!" she moaned. "There's nothing about the curse in *any* of these books."

Joe shut his book. "I don't think there's anything about it in this one, either," he said.

Nothing else had gone wrong since the hut collapsed. Still, Michelle wasn't taking any chances. She and Joe were searching through Ken's books on Hawaiian folklore for any mention of the Curse of the Green Lagoon.

"Maybe we should call Ken and ask him about it," Michelle suggested.

"Can't. Ken flew to the Big Island. His niece is getting married there this weekend," Joe explained. "Which means he won't be back until next Monday." He paused. "What do we do now?"

I want to go home to San Francisco and pretend none of this ever happened, Michelle thought. Running away wasn't going to get rid of the curse, though.

"We need facts," Michelle reasoned. "And we're not finding them in these books. So maybe we need to get our information from some other place!"

Joe gave her a puzzled glance. "You mean, you want to go to a library?"

"No. I mean, we could try to find the guy who told you about the curse in the first place," Michelle said.

"I already asked my dad if he knew where Dr. Matson was," Joe told her. "He said he's back at the dig, where his team is looking for bones."

Michelle crossed her fingers. She hoped the dig wasn't on one of the other islands. "Does your dad know where the dig is?"

"Yeah," Joe said. "It's in the palm forest, not far from the Hawaiian Hideaway."

"Where's that?" Michelle asked. "Can we go there now?"

"No way," Joe said. "The resort is pretty close. But the dig is in the forest. And I'm not allowed to go there alone."

Michelle scowled. This was a problem. A big problem.

"We have to do something," she muttered. "We can't just sit around and let the curse get stronger and stronger."

"It will keep on getting stronger until the full moon," Joe reminded her.

"When is the full moon, anyway?" Michelle wondered.

Joe swallowed. "Friday."

"But this is Wednesday afternoon!" Michelle gasped. "Friday is the day after tomorrow!"

There was no time to waste. She thought hard, then snapped her fingers.

"I know!" she exclaimed. "We'll get Stephanie to take us to the dig."

"But she'll never believe there's really a curse on you," Joe warned.

"That's okay. We just won't tell her that part," Michelle promised. "All I have to do is get her to take us there tomorrow. Before things get *really* bad!"

"I'm sorry, Michelle, but I can't take you to the dig site." Stephanie settled down on her own bed. "Why don't you spend the day at the beach instead?"

"No!" Michelle practically screamed.

Stephanie looked at her in surprise.

"I mean, I'd rather see the archaeological site with you," Michelle said quickly.

"Sorry," Stephanie explained. "Maybe on Saturday we could go."

"Saturday is too late!" Michelle told her.

"Why?" Stephanie wondered.

Michelle thought fast. "Um—the doctor told me to keep my rash out of the sun. So I really shouldn't go to the beach tomorrow. I really should stay under some palm trees, and the dig is in the trees."

Stephanie squinted at Michelle. "I can barely see your rash. It looks totally better."

"I know." Michelle glanced down at her

bare arms and legs. The rash was practically gone. The ointment the doctor had given her really cleared things up. "But Dad wants me to be careful, too. Why can't you just take me and Joe for a walk tomorrow?"

"Because . . . tomorrow I'm not going anywhere near the palm forest," her sister explained. "I've decided to—uh—to take a walk on my own. Over to the grotto Mr. Grant told us about. On the other side of the island."

Michelle gave Stephanie her best pleading look. "But, Stephanie, this might be our only chance to see a real archaeologists' dig. It will be very . . . educational!"

"Since when do you want an educational vacation?" Stephanie asked.

"Uh . . . since Joe told me about it," Michelle replied. "And I've been reading books about the history of the island and everything! I mean, since I had to stay indoors."

Stephanie gave her a sympathetic smile. "Sorry, Michelle. No can do."

Michelle sighed in frustration. She couldn't give up. She had to talk to Dr. Matson. He might be the only one who knew how to stop the curse—before something really terrible happened.

"Please," Michelle begged. "You'll love the dig! It's better than anything you'd see at the grotto!"

"I can't go, Michelle!" Stephanie snapped. "I've got everyone counting on—" She stopped suddenly. Her cheeks turned red.

Michelle knew that look. It was the way Stephanie always looked when she was trying to hide something.

"Who is *everyone?*" Michelle asked.

"Umm—these kids I met yesterday. They said they might go to the grotto and—"

Bingo! Michelle thought. Stephanie's eyes nearly crossed, she was trying so hard to act innocent. She definitely had some kind of secret.

Michelle grinned. "You might as well tell me the truth," she said. "I know you're hiding something. So spill."

"Okay, okay," Stephanie muttered. She glared at Michelle, then took a deep breath. "The truth is, I'm not going for a nature walk. I'm going to the Hawaiian Hideaway to take hula lessons."

"You're kidding!" Michelle said. "The dig is in the forest right near the Hawaiian Hideaway. This is perfect! You can take Joe and me there before your hula lesson. Then I could watch you take your class!"

"Forget that, Michelle," Stephanie told her. "*I'm* not even supposed to be there. The lessons are supposed to be only for guests at the hotel."

Michelle held up her right hand. "I promise I won't tell anyone we're staying here. Come on, Steph. Please?"

"Oh, all right," Stephanie agreed. She went over to the dresser. She picked a pink hibiscus from the vase, tucked it behind her ear, and studied her reflection in the mirror. "But we have to leave in time for me to get to my class."

"No problem," Michelle promised.

"And remember—Dad can't know why I'm really going over there," Stephanie said. She made a face. "I can't believe you know the truth."

"Don't worry. Your secret's totally safe with me," Michelle assured her.

She breathed a sigh of relief. Tomorrow she and Joe would talk to Dr. Matson, and they'd find out how to stop the curse!

She gave a happy little bounce on the bed—and heard a loud *craaack!*

Stephanie whirled around. "What was that?"

Michelle checked under the bed. One of the bed's wooden legs had a wide split running up it. One more bounce, and it would break!

"It's nothing," she said quickly. Inside, though, she knew what really had happened. It was the curse! she realized. It had nearly struck again!

On Thursday morning Michelle woke up feeling totally excited. *Today we are sure to find Dr. Matson*, she thought. *My bad luck will disappear—and I'll be a normal kid again!*

Of course, something awful could still happen *before* she got to the dig. Which meant that they'd better get to the palm forest ASAP.

She bolted out of bed and hurried into the bathroom. She quickly scrubbed her face and brushed her teeth.

She dressed neatly in a pink T-shirt, white shorts, and her bright pink sneakers. She needed to make a good impression on Dr. Matson.

Michelle heard Stephanie yawn and turned to see her sitting up in bed, stretching.

"Time to get up," Michelle told her.

Stephanie flung her blanket aside and headed to the bathroom to wash up. "Relax, Michelle," she told her. "We have plenty of time."

Half an hour later Stephanie and Michelle stepped out of their hut. Together they crossed the clearing toward the dining room.

Their dad appeared at the doorway to his hut, right ahead of them. He too was dressed and ready for breakfast.

"Good morning, girls," Danny called to them.

"Good morning, Dad," they replied.

"Hurry up, Steph," Michelle told her. "We don't want to be late for your hul—"

Stephanie shot her a quick warning look.

"For your *hot* breakfast," Michelle quickly said.

"Hot breakfast on a ninety-degree day?" Danny asked. He chuckled.

"Well, I know how much you believe in good nutrition," Michelle told him.

"I think cold cereal will be fine today," Danny replied. He grinned as he entered the dining room ahead of them.

"Whew!" Michelle muttered. "That was a close one!"

"Too close," Stephanie whispered. She looked angry. "You'd better be careful, Michelle. I don't know what will happen if you spill the beans."

"Don't worry. From now on my lips are sealed!" Michelle mimed locking her lips and throwing away the key. She knew she had to be very careful. Until that curse was removed, *anything* could go wrong.

After breakfast Michelle and Stephanie met Joe in front of the office hut. Joe handed Stephanie a piece of paper. "My dad drew a map to help us find the dig," he explained.

Stephanie led the way along the beach and into the palm forest. Michelle kept her eyes wide open as they walked along the shaded path. Who knew when a tree would fall or a coconut would drop—right on top of her!

After a while they heard voices ahead of them.

"That must be it!" Michelle said.

She broke into a run. She was the first one to reach the clearing, where several men were gathered around a hole in the ground. Her sister and Joe joined her seconds later.

"This is what you were so excited to see?" Stephanie asked Michelle. "I've got to tell you—it's just a big hole in the ground!"

"But my dad told me they found something really important here," Joe said. "Some giant bones. They think they're from some kind of prehistoric creature."

"I guess that's pretty cool," Stephanie admitted. She stepped closer to the hole to get a good look.

"I want to see, too," Joe said.

Michelle sighed. All she wanted to do was talk to Dr. Matson. But since she was there, she might as well see what was going on.

She leaned over the edge of the hole. Two more men stood inside it. Together they were slowly lifting up the biggest bone she'd ever seen.

She shifted her foot, trying to get a better look. A stone popped loose from beneath her sneaker.

It tumbled into the pit—and hit one of the men on his neck!

"What was that?" The man looked around in surprise—and dropped his end of the gigantic bone.

Ping!

Michelle watched a long crack snake along the bone!

The scientists gasped. Some of them groaned.

Michelle groaned, too. It was just like what happened with the bed last night. The curse had struck again!

She dropped her head into her hands. "What have I done now?" she murmured.

"What are you kids doing here?" one of the scientists asked.

"We just came to see the dig," Stephanie answered.

Joe tapped Michelle on the arm. "I think we'd better find Dr. Matson," he whispered. "Quick."

"No kidding!" Michelle whispered back. They had to end this curse fast!

While her sister talked to the other scientists, Michelle walked up to a man who stood by himself. He was writing on a clipboard.

"Excuse me," she said. "But we're looking for Dr. Matson. Is that you?"

The man smiled down at her. "I'm afraid Dr. Matson isn't here. He went to the mainland. He needed to discuss our find with some other scientists."

"When is he coming back?" Michelle asked. "It's really, really important that we see him."

"Oh, he's not coming back," the man said. "His job here is done now. He's gone."

"Gone?" Michelle turned to Joe in dismay. "Now what will we do?"

STEPHANIE

Chapter
11

Stephanie glanced at her watch. Hula class began in exactly fifteen minutes. They were just about out of the palm forest, but the Hawaiian Hideaway still wasn't in sight. Michelle and Joe were inching along like snails!

"Come on, you guys," Stephanie called. She turned around to look at the two younger kids. "What's got you so upset?" she asked. "You were so excited to go to the dig. And now that you've gone . . . you both look like you're miserable!"

"You wouldn't understand," Joe told her.

Moments later the hotel came into sight. "My dad is cool with me walking back from here on my own," Joe told Stephanie. "Thanks for taking us to the dig."

"What about you, Michelle?" Stephanie asked. "Do you want to go back with Joe or stay with me?"

Michelle shrugged. "Doesn't matter," she said in a flat voice.

Stephanie debated silently. *My secret is a lot safer if Michelle goes back to the Haven with Joe,* she realized. *But something's got Michelle upset. I can't send her away now!*

"You need some cheering up," Stephanie decided. "You're staying with me."

Michelle shrugged again. "See you later," she said to Joe. She glanced around. "If I don't get caught in a tidal wave or something first."

Joe gave her a worried look and started off to the Haven.

Stephanie put an arm around her sister's shoulder. "Wait until you see the Hawaiian Hideaway. It's beautiful. And a pineapple-coconut smoothie is sure to cheer you up in no time."

Stephanie led Michelle along the cove and up the pink stairs to the low pool.

"Wow!" Michelle's eyes lit up. "A beach, two pools, and a river! This place is amazing!"

"Tell me about it! Just remember," Stephanie added in a whisper, "if anyone asks, we're guests here!"

"I wish!" Michelle exclaimed. Stephanie shot her a look.

"Got it!" Michelle whispered back.

Stephanie pointed ahead of them. "Those are my friends."

Amber, Molly, and Patricia sat on the lawn near the really fancy wing of the hotel.

"Amber!" Stephanie called. "Hey, you guys!"

Amber and the others smiled as Stephanie headed toward them.

"This is my sister, Michelle," Stephanie said.

"Hi, Michelle!" Amber gave her a huge smile. Molly and Patricia greeted her, too.

"Let's head over to the pavilion," Stephanie suggested. "I really would like to practice a bit before our lesson."

"We can't. We promised to wait here for Laura," Amber said. "She ran back to her room to get her sunglasses."

"Too bad she's staying in that back wing," Patricia added. "It's so far away from everything."

Laura smiled at Michelle. "So how do you like your suite?"

"Our suite?" Michelle echoed.

Stephanie gently elbowed her sister.

"Oh, our *suite*," Michelle said quickly. "It's great. I mean, it's so—big. And pretty. It's amazing," she babbled on. "You have to see it to believe it!"

"Hey, that's a good idea, Michelle! Why don't you guys take us on a tour of your place?" Patricia said.

Ugh! Stephanie wished she could clamp a hand over her sister's mouth. *Good going, Michelle,* she thought. *Now what do I do?*

"Hey, here comes Laura," Amber said.

Saved! Stephanie thought. *Now we can all just go over to the dance pavilion.*

Molly glanced at her watch. "We've still got ten minutes before class starts," she said.

"What do you think, Stephanie? Want to show us around your suite?"

Stephanie forced herself to look calm. "Uh—sure," she answered. "We just have to check that it's okay with my dad first."

She pulled Michelle through one of the doors to the hotel. They stood in the hall where Stephanie had seen that beautiful suite the day before. The suite that was supposed to be hers!

"I thought you promised to keep this a secret!" she whispered.

"I was trying to!" Michelle said. "All that stuff just slipped out. I guess I got carried away."

"Great. Now what am I going to do?" Stephanie slumped back against the wall.

"Hello, again!"

Stephanie looked up and saw the chambermaid she'd met the day before. The girl pushed a huge cart filled with cleaning supplies. It was packed with a vacuum, a duster, sponges, brushes, cleansing powders, and stacks of plastic garbage bags.

"Hi, there!" Stephanie said.

The girl unlocked the door to the same suite Stephanie had been inside. "This cart weighs a ton. Would you mind holding the door open for a second?" she asked.

"No problem," Stephanie replied. Hmmm. This gave her an idea.

She held the door. The girl wheeled the cart into the suite.

Stephanie peered into the living room. It looked empty.

"Excuse me," she said. "But is anybody staying in here?"

"Not anymore," the girl answered. "They checked out this morning. The next guests aren't arriving until this evening."

Stephanie felt like cheering. What a stroke of good luck!

"Could you do me a little favor?" she asked the chambermaid. "My friends are dying to see this suite. Can I just show it to them? It will take only a minute."

The girl shrugged. "I guess that's okay," she said. "I can start on the suite next door instead. And I'll leave this door open for you. Look all you want. Just don't touch anything."

"We won't," Stephanie promised. She turned to Michelle. "Go get Amber and the others," she ordered.

Stephanie helped the chambermaid get the cart into the next suite.

She was gazing out at the balcony when Michelle returned with the other girls.

"Wow!" Laura said. "Michelle is right. This room is gorgeous!"

"And look at this!" Molly called from the bathroom. "A Jacuzzi in the tub *and* a TV you can watch while you're soaking! I wish I could have a bubble bath right now!"

"Yeah, but the bathroom TV isn't as big as this wide-screen television in the living room," Patricia added. "This is like having your own private movie theater!"

"Boy, you guys sure keep this place neat," Amber remarked.

"Yeah, it's almost like no one is staying here," Molly agreed.

"Uh—my family is incredibly tidy," Stephanie replied. She'd been wondering if anyone would notice that there were no clothes or personal belongings around.

"She's right," Michelle added. "Our dad's a total neat freak."

"Well, we'd better go," Stephanie said. She had to get out of there before the chambermaid returned—and before Michelle said anything else that got her into a jam. "We don't want to be late for our lesson."

"Okay. But it's too bad we didn't get to check out a movie on that wide-screen TV," Amber said.

"Maybe later," Michelle said politely.

Stephanie gave her another elbow in the shoulder. Was she really inviting the girls to a room that wasn't theirs *again*?

Michelle's blue eyes widened. "Oops!" she whispered.

One hour later Stephanie stepped off the stage. Her muscles ached, but she felt good. The class had gone really well. And it looked as if everyone had forgotten about Michelle's invitation.

"Well, time to go," Stephanie called. She grabbed Michelle. "See you guys later." She definitely had to get back to the Haven before her sister got her into even more trouble.

"Wait, Steph!" Amber said. "How about catching that movie in your room now?"

Stephanie shot Michelle a look of panic. No way could they get back into the hotel room! If she tried, she'd be totally exposed. What was she going to do?

"Uh, that'd be fun," Stephanie began. "But, uh, we can't. Because—I forgot my keys." She pretended to search through her pockets. "I left them back in the suite. We're locked out."

Michelle slapped a hand on her forehead. "Wow! I forgot *my* keys, too!" she exclaimed.

"And I just remembered that our whole family is out. They won't be back until way after dinner," Stephanie added. "So we'll just have to make it another day."

"Too bad." Patricia shrugged. "Come on, guys. Let's go swimming instead."

"Have fun," Stephanie said. She grabbed Michelle's arm. "I think it's safer for us to get out of here," she whispered. "I'm afraid we'll get into more trouble if we stick around."

"What will you tell your friends?" Michelle asked.

"I'll just say I'm taking you on a nature walk," Stephanie replied. "A very long nature walk."

"Hey, Stephanie, wait!" Amber ran toward them. "I just had a great idea. I'll find a chambermaid to let you into your room. They all carry keys."

"Really, don't do that," Stephanie said. "I don't want you to go to all that trouble."

"It's no trouble at all." Amber hurried off to find a chambermaid.

Stephanie watched her go. The other girls were still heading toward the pool. She groaned. "Michelle, I think we're about to be busted!"

"What should we do?" Michelle asked.

"There's only one thing to do in a situation like this," Stephanie told her. "Run!"

Chapter
12

Michelle and Stephanie kept running all the way back to the Haven. Michelle reached the clearing first.

"Stop!" She bent over and took a few deep breaths. "We're safe now, Steph."

Stephanie slowed to a walk. She gasped for air. "Well, at least we got away," she finally said.

"Yeah," Michelle agreed. "But how will you explain it to your friends tomorrow? Won't they want to know *why* we ran off that way?"

Stephanie thought for a minute. "I'll say I suddenly realized I lost my keys on the beach.

So we ran off to look for them and didn't have time to tell anyone."

Michelle nodded. "Sounds good."

Stephanie frowned. "Well, I'd better go change. See you at dinner."

I've got to find Joe, Michelle realized. *We have to figure out another way to stop the curse.*

She found Joe in the hotel office. He sat in Ken Takei's chair. His feet were up on the desk, and he was reading a thick blue book.

"Michelle!" Joe held up the book. "I think I found it!"

"You actually found something about the Curse of the Green Lagoon?" Michelle asked. Her heart started to hammer with excitement.

"Not exactly," Joe admitted. "But it has a page about how to remove a curse—any curse."

"Do you think it will work on mine?"

Joe shrugged. "It can't hurt to try. And it's all we've got."

"True." Michelle wasn't going to hesitate. "Let's try it now."

Joe gazed around the office. "I don't think this is the best place for that," he said. "My dad might walk in on us and wonder what we're doing. Besides, this book says you're supposed to go to the ocean to remove the curse. The water helps carry it away. . . . Wait a minute." He snapped his fingers. "I know just the place."

He led Michelle down to a deserted stretch of beach. "Let's go over near that big black rock," Joe said. "Nobody ever goes there."

They settled into the shade behind the giant rock. A dark cloud suddenly covered the clear sky. Michelle shivered. She hoped this wasn't going to be scary.

Joe opened the book again. He scanned the page. "Here it is," he said. He handed the book to Michelle.

Michelle read aloud, " 'Removing a curse can be difficult. It takes great concentration. . . .' " She read farther down the page. "It says I'm supposed to concentrate really hard, say these words, then offer a gift to the ocean. What does that mean?"

"I think it means you throw some bread into the water or something," Joe guessed.

Michelle shook her head. This wasn't very

logical at all. "What's the ocean going to do with soggy bread?" she asked.

Joe raised his hands in the air. "I don't know! Maybe the fish will eat it. But we don't have any bread here. So how about"—he turned his pockets inside out—"half a granola bar?"

"Yuck," Michelle said. "I sure hope the ocean isn't fussy about what you offer it."

Michelle set the book down on the beach and concentrated really hard. She raised her arms and recited the words in the book, which really sounded like a bunch of nonsense. Then she flung the granola bar into the waves. "Take the curse—and this granola bar—away from me!" she shouted.

"Are you done?" Joe asked.

"Yeah. But I don't know if anything happened," Michelle said. "I didn't feel anything. Did you?"

"Nope. And I didn't hear anything except the ocean," Joe added.

Michelle frowned.

"Wait a minute," Joe said suddenly. "You know what? I think it did work!"

Michelle looked at him in disbelief. "What makes you so sure?"

Joe pointed to the sky. "When you started saying those words, the sky was really dark. And now the sun's out again. That must mean that the darkness of the curse has been lifted from you!"

Michelle suddenly felt light and happy inside. "Hey! You're right!" she said. "We got rid of the curse! Let's go back to the Haven and celebrate."

They walked around the big rock. Michelle spotted Danny on the beach up ahead. He wore baggy swim trunks and carried a surfboard.

"Dad! What's up?" she called. She and Joe hurried closer.

Danny turned toward them. He looked very worried. "Uncle Jesse and I were surfing together," he began. "Then the strangest thing happened. The tide got really strong. I made it back to shore. But I lost sight of Jesse. I was just looking for him."

Gulp. Uncle Jesse was *missing?*

Michelle clutched Joe's arm. "Oh, no. Are

you thinking what I'm thinking?" she whispered.

Joe shot her a look of panic. "You mean that maybe I was wrong," he whispered back. "That maybe the curse didn't go away after all."

Michelle bit her lip. That's *exactly* what she had been thinking. She and Joe walked behind Danny as he searched the beach.

"There he is!" Danny exclaimed.

Michelle saw her uncle wading through the low surf. He was dragging his surfboard with one hand. He looked completely worn out.

"Jesse! Over here!" Danny called. He strode toward Jesse. Michelle and Joe followed close behind.

"Am I glad to see you guys!" Jesse dropped the surfboard. He took big gulps of air.

"What happened to you?" Danny asked. "You disappeared. I got really worried."

"It was strange," Jesse told him. "I caught a wave to follow you into shore. But instead, it pushed me out beyond that rock." Jesse pointed to the big rock where Michelle and Joe had gone to remove the curse.

"I kept trying to paddle away from the rock," Jesse went on. "But no matter how hard I tried, I couldn't get anywhere. It was totally weird. It almost felt as if something were holding me back."

"Wow! I felt the same way!" Danny exclaimed. "How did you finally break away?"

"I'm not sure how, but I'm glad I did." Jesse chuckled. "Sounds like something out of a dumb horror movie, huh? Mysterious force captures surfers!"

Danny laughed. "I'm just glad you're all right," he said. "I was really scared for a minute, buddy."

"Me, too," Jesse admitted. "Now I'm just tired. Let's head back to the Haven."

Jesse picked up his surfboard. He and Danny walked slowly up the beach.

Michelle held her breath until they had disappeared in the distance.

"Did you hear that?" she asked Joe. Her voice came out tight and squeaky. Her heart pounded. Her palms felt clammy.

Joe's face was pale. He looked as scared as Michelle felt.

"I heard," he said in a small voice. "A mysterious force got them."

"There's no mystery about it," Michelle said. "It was the curse. And it's getting stronger!"

"What do we do now?" Joe asked.

"The full moon's tomorrow. If we don't find a cure by then, there's only one thing we can do," Michelle said. "Protect my family from the curse the best way we can."

"*Everyone* in your family?" Joe asked. "That's a lot of people to keep track of."

Michelle thought for a moment. Joe was right—she certainly couldn't keep track of six people at once. Maybe she should concentrate on a few people in particular.

Let's see, the twins and Aunt Becky lost their lunch because of the curse. Uncle Jesse and her father had nearly been swept out to sea. Michelle had already had a terrible rash. That left—

"Oh, no!" Michelle gasped. "The only person in my family who hasn't been affected by the curse is—Stephanie!"

Chapter
13

Stephanie jumped and let out a little yelp as the door to her hut slammed open. Michelle burst in.

"There you are!" Michelle panted. "And you're all right!"

"I *was* all right until you nearly scared me half to death," Stephanie snapped. "What's wrong with you, Michelle?"

"Oh, nothing." Michelle dropped onto Stephanie's bed. She shoved aside a pile of magazines, hair clips, brushes, and combs.

"What are you doing?" Stephanie asked. "Can't you see I'm using those?"

"Oh. Sorry. I, uh, I just wanted to be near you," Michelle said.

"What?" Stephanie straightened out her beauty supplies. Then she looked more closely at her sister. "Michelle, is everything okay?"

"Fine. Everything's totally fine," Michelle answered.

"Well, then, calm down, okay? And please don't sit on my scrunchies. I'm trying to figure out the perfect hairdo for the luau tomorrow."

Stephanie twisted her hair into a loose bun and checked it out in the mirror. Not bad. But not great.

"The luau?" Michelle repeated.

"Yeah," Stephanie said. "I want to look great for my big hula number."

She also wanted to look great for Lonnie, but she wasn't about to tell Michelle about that.

She grabbed her brush and smoothed out her hair. Actually, she wished Michelle didn't know anything about the luau. Or the hula performance. It was hard enough for Stephanie to keep her secret on her own. The fact that Michelle knew about it too made her nervous.

It's only for one more day, Stephanie reminded herself. *Then I can tell everyone the truth—and hope like mad that they won't think I'm a total loser afterward.*

Stephanie worked her hair into a French braid. She checked her reflection in the dresser mirror. No, that wasn't right. Too French, not Hawaiian enough. She loosened the braid and brushed her hair out again.

"Ow!" she cried.

"What?" Michelle was at her side in an instant. "What's wrong? Are you okay?"

"I had a knot in my hair," Stephanie explained. "I'm fine."

"Good!" Michelle looked relieved, but she didn't move.

"Uh, Michelle?" Stephanie said. "Togetherness is nice and all. But could you give me a little space?"

Michelle backed off.

Stephanie shook her head. She certainly had enough to think about without her little sister getting underfoot.

"Don't you have someplace to go?" she asked.

"No place at all," Michelle told her.

"Too bad," Stephanie muttered. She reached for a glittery comb on the dresser. Her hairbrush slipped out of her hand.

"Watch it!" Michelle dived to the floor. She scooped up the hairbrush and held it as if it were going to explode.

"It's just a hairbrush, Michelle." Stephanie stared at her sister. "You know, the way you're acting is really freaking me out here."

Michelle silently handed Stephanie the brush.

Stephanie swept her hair into a loose twist. She secured it with one of her hair clips. There. That was how she'd wear it! Now she was totally looking forward to tomorrow night.

It's going to be okay, she told herself. *I'm doing the right thing. I'm not going to let down Lonnie or Mahina or Amber or the others. No one will find out I'm not really a guest at the Hawaiian Hideaway. It's all going to work out.*

She glanced at her wristwatch. It was

nearly dinner time! "Are you coming to the dining hut?" she asked Michelle. "I'm starving."

"If you're going, I'm going, too," Michelle said.

"Weird," Stephanie murmured. "Totally weird."

They hurried to the dining hut. Joe and his dad were already seated at the table. Danny had invited the two of them to join the Tanners for dinner.

"I wanted to thank Joe and his dad for making our stay so pleasant," Danny explained. He beamed at them. "Becky and I haven't felt this relaxed in months."

He turned to Stephanie and Michelle. "You two look pretty relaxed, too," he said. "Not to mention healthy. I guess going on that nature walk was really good for you."

Stephanie felt a pang of guilt. *Actually, hula lessons and the friends I've made at the Hawaiian Hideaway have been good for me*, she thought.

Danny raised his glass for a toast. "To this week—a total success," he declared. "In fact, I think this calls for a special family celebration."

"Ice cream!" Nicky suggested.

"No, cotton candy," Alex argued.

Danny smiled. "Actually," he said, "I was thinking we might have a picnic on the beach. Tomorrow evening! We'll have a celebration supper under the full moon."

Stephanie stared at her father in horror. *A family picnic? Friday evening!* She couldn't. That was when she was supposed to be at the luau! That was when she was supposed to be performing!

"That's a great idea!" Becky said.

"What do you think, guys?" Jesse asked the twins.

Everyone started talking at once. From what Stephanie could tell, she was the only one who wasn't thrilled with the idea. She had to do something—fast!

"Uh, Dad," she interrupted. "I have an even better idea." She flashed a bright smile. "Why don't you guys have an adults-only evening instead?"

"What do you mean, Steph?"

"Michelle and I will watch the twins," Stephanie went on. "You guys can go out and do adult stuff. You deserve it," she added.

Actually Michelle would watch the twins, Stephanie thought. Then she could sneak away to the luau.

Danny looked totally surprised—and pleased. "Wow, Steph. That sounds great. But I can't ask you to give up your whole evening for us."

"Why not?" Stephanie argued. "We can have fun on our own."

"It's okay with me," Michelle said.

"Well, *I* say, let's go for it," Jesse said. "There are a couple of hot music spots that I've been wanting to check out."

Becky put an arm around her husband. "And a few restaurants *I've* been wanting to check out."

Danny laughed. "Okay. It's settled, then. Adults' night out on Friday."

Stephanie let out a sigh of relief.

That was close! she thought. But now she was all set. She could definitely go to the luau!

As soon as dinner was over, she hurried back to her hut. She wanted to practice her solo dance.

Michelle followed closely behind.

Stephanie rolled her eyes. A little sisterly to-getherness was nice, but this was getting ridiculous. Maybe if she just ignored Michelle, her sister would get the message and leave her alone.

Stephanie positioned herself in front of the mirror and tied a flowered skirt around her waist. It wasn't exactly a grass skirt, but it would do.

She hummed the opening notes from her dance and lifted her arms.

"Uh, Steph . . . about tomorrow night—" Michelle began.

Stephanie sighed. "Can't this wait? You see I'm rehearsing."

"No, Steph, it can't wait!" Michelle sounded almost hysterical.

Stephanie put her arms down and turned to face her sister.

"Okay," Stephanie said. "Here's the plan. As you know, I need to go to the luau tomorrow night. So if you and Joe stay here and watch the twins, I'll make sure you guys have plenty of snacks and stuff. I mean, I don't want you to feel like you're missing out on anything. Okay?"

"No!" Michelle said.

"No?" Stephanie couldn't believe what she was hearing. "Michelle, you know how important the luau is to me."

She thought quickly, then added, "What if I give you a week's allowance when we get back to San Francisco?"

"Stephanie, I can't let you do that!" Michelle wailed.

"What do you mean, you can't?" Stephanie had to force herself to sound calm. "I have been looking forward to tomorrow night all week! Look, I'm really sorry if it seems like I'm the only one who'll be having a good time, but—"

"Just trust me on this," Michelle pleaded. "You absolutely, positively *cannot* go to that luau tomorrow night!"

Chapter 14

Stephanie stared at Michelle in shock. "What is wrong with you?" she demanded. "Of course I'm going to the luau! Why on earth wouldn't I?"

Michelle swallowed hard. She had to warn Stephanie. To tell her that something terrible might happen at the luau. But how?

She could hardly start talking about evil spirits and curses. Stephanie would think she was totally, completely crazy.

Oh, man! Michelle thought. *Protecting Stephanie is not going to be easy.*

Michelle took a deep breath. "Stephanie, I've kept your secret about the hula lessons," she began. "And I'll go on keeping it—on one condition. You have to let *me* come to the luau tomorrow night."

"What?" Stephanie shrieked. "No way, Michelle! This is my big evening. Besides, you have to watch the twins."

"Joe will come with us. We'll both watch the twins—at the luau," Michelle said. She stubbornly crossed her arms. "The way I see it, you don't have a choice. If you go to the luau, we *all* go to the luau."

"What a pain," Stephanie muttered. "But there's no time to argue. Okay, you can come. But you'd better take really, really good care of the twins. And stay out of my way!"

I'll take good care of the twins, Michelle agreed silently. *But I'm not staying out of your way. In fact, I plan to stick close to you all evening. Very, very close!*

Friday evening was warm and lovely. The sky was clear. The air smelled of hibiscus and jasmine flowers.

If Michelle didn't already know the danger Stephanie was in, she might actually enjoy it.

Problems in Paradise

"What a gorgeous night!" Aunt Becky exclaimed. The family had gathered in the dining hut before separating for their big night out. Becky wore a pretty flowered dress. Even Uncle Jesse, who almost always dressed casually, was wearing a linen shirt and a jacket with his jeans.

"The sky is so clear, I think the light of the full moon will be especially powerful tonight," Mr. Grant told them.

Michelle exchanged a look of horror with Joe. Did that mean the curse would be even stronger?

"Well, we're leaving," Danny said. "You kids have fun!"

"We will," Stephanie answered.

Yeah, sure, Michelle added silently. *Fun.*

"Okay, I'm ready to go," Stephanie told Michelle as soon as the adults were on their way. "Are you and the twins ready to leave?"

Michelle swallowed hard. "I guess so," she answered.

"We need to get going early so I can find Amber and the others," Stephanie explained. "We planned to practice together one last time before the performance."

Michelle watched Stephanie with a sinking feeling. They had fought plenty of times, but Michelle loved her sister. She didn't want her to be hurt by this stupid curse!

Michelle glanced at Joe. "Are you ready to go?" she asked.

Joe nodded. Then Stephanie, Michelle, Joe, and the twins all set off for the Hawaiian Hideaway.

Ten minutes later, Michelle studied the beach in front of the resort. Brightly colored lanterns were strung from palm tree to palm tree. Garlands of beautiful flowers decorated the outdoor pavilions. Long banquet tables were piled high with delicious fruits and platters of food. Smaller tables held snacks and pitchers of ice-cold tropical drinks. Chairs, and even a few hammocks, were set up around the dance pavilion.

"We want a hammock!" Nicky declared.

"Good idea," Joe said. "Let's go get you one."

Four musicians tuned up their instruments on a bandstand next to the dance pavilion. Guests strolled the beach, talking and laughing. They were already having a wonderful time.

Michelle and Joe settled the twins in a hammock. Michelle began to rock them. She smiled as the boys' eyes began to drift shut. Her little cousins were bundles of energy one second, sound asleep the next.

"Michelle, look!" Joe pointed up at the sky. The full moon shone high over the ocean.

Michelle's eyes darted to the stage. There was no sign of the hula dancers yet. They were probably still practicing. But Michelle decided that once Stephanie showed up, she wouldn't take her eyes off her. Or better yet . . .

"I have an idea!" Michelle told Joe. "Maybe we can stop the hula performance! I can protect Stephanie from the curse better if she's not onstage."

"That's true. But how are you going to stop the show?" Joe asked.

"I don't know," she admitted. "Watch the twins for a few minutes. I'll try to figure something out."

Joe glanced at the moon again. "Go for it!" he told her.

Michelle decided to check out the stage area. She wasn't sure what she was looking for, but she hoped to see something that would give her an idea.

Maybe I could get a platter of food and manage to spill it all over the stage, she thought. *No, someone would just mop it up, and the show would go on.*

Thinking hard, she circled around the back of the stage—a square platform that was open on all four sides. She picked her way through a tangle of electric cords that led from the instruments to the stage. Then she spotted a large cardboard box.

Michelle kneeled down and opened the lid. "Bingo!" she whispered. The box was filled with grass hula skirts. All she had to do was get rid of the skirts. Then Stephanie and the others wouldn't be able to dance!

The question was, where could she hide them? Michelle glanced around. She spied a big black case tucked behind the bandstand. Michelle went over to investigate.

I sure hope no one notices me, she thought as she opened the latch on the case. Luckily, the musicians were busy running a sound check on their instruments.

Michelle saw that the inside of the case was

empty. *This must have held one of the instruments,* she realized. *And now it will be the perfect place for these hula skirts!*

Quickly Michelle stuffed the hula skirts in the big black case. Then she sneaked back to Joe and the twins.

"Mission accomplished!" she told him.

"What'd you do?" he asked.

Michelle leaned close to whisper, "I hid the hula skirts! Now they can't possibly dance."

Joe grinned and gave her a thumbs-up.

"Michelle!" someone called.

Michelle nearly jumped a foot in the air. She whirled around. Mahina walked toward her. She wore a grass skirt, a colorful lei, and lots of flowers in her dark hair.

"I'm so glad you could come tonight," the hula teacher said. "Have you seen a big cardboard box anywhere? I was sure it was right back here. It has our grass skirts for the performance."

Michelle knew she couldn't look at the hula teacher without giving herself away. So she looked around instead. "I don't see it anywhere," she told Mahina.

"Oh, well. No matter," Mahina answered. "I

have some extras stored in the hotel office. Guess I'd better go get them. Enjoy the show, Michelle!"

Michelle felt sick to her stomach. *It's that rotten curse!* she thought. *It won't even give me a chance to stop it!*

"Looks like the performance is back on," she reported to Joe.

"No kidding." He nodded toward the hotel. Stephanie and her friends were walking toward the stage. They wore beautiful flower leis—and grass skirts.

Michelle thought her sister looked beautiful. She would be really happy for her—if she weren't so worried!

Mahina stepped onstage and took the mike. "Attention, everyone!" The crowd quieted down. "Tonight, we're proud to present a performance by the Hawaiian Hideaway's own hula class. Please give a warm welcome to Amber, Molly, Laura, Patricia, and our lead dancer—Stephanie!"

The musicians began to play. The hula class stepped onto the stage. The audience began to applaud.

Michelle groaned. Somehow, she'd have to

guard Stephanie against the curse while she was onstage.

The twins woke up and cheered. "Cousin Stephie! Cousin Stephie!" The two boys jumped out of the hammock.

"Hey!" Michelle called.

Before she could catch them, Nicky and Alex sprinted through the crowd. They were headed straight for the stage!

Michelle took off after the twins. "Nicky, Alex, come back here!" she shouted.

Joe jogged past her. Onstage the dancers took their places and the curtain closed in front of them.

"Before we begin," Mahina said, "I'd like to explain a little about hula dancing so that you'll understand the meaning of the dances you're about to see."

Oh, no! Michelle saw Alex head for the stairs that led to the stage. Joe caught him just in time! But as Joe swung Alex into his arms, Nicky darted around them—to the area behind the stage.

Michelle raced after Nicky. She crouched down so that no one would see her back there.

Mahina finished demonstrating a series of graceful arm movements. Then the curtain parted, and Stephanie and her friends began to dance.

Nicky made a beeline for the back of the stage.

"Nicky, slow down!" Michelle whispered.

He climbed on top of a crate that someone had set against the stage platform.

Michelle was only a few feet away from him now. "Nicky!" she repeated.

She snatched him up in her arms—and stopped. Something had caught her eye. The metal rod that ran high across the performers—the rod for the stage curtain.

One of the sandbags that helped balance the curtain hung from the center of the rod.

Michelle blinked hard. No, she wasn't imagining it. The sandbag's rope was fraying. And the heavy sandbag hung directly over Stephanie!

The music stopped for a moment, and the beat of the drum quickened. The rest of the hula students stepped back, and Stephanie began her solo dance.

Michelle's eyes darted back and forth between Stephanie and the sandbag's fraying rope. *Any minute now, that sandbag is going to come down on my sister's head!* she realized. She had to do something to save her—and she had to do it now.

"Don't move, Nicky!" Michelle ordered. Then she took a deep breath. "Watch out, Steph!" she cried.

Michelle ran onto the stage—and tackled her sister.

"Ooof!" Stephanie gasped. The two girls fell to the floor.

"Michelle!" Stephanie yelled. "Have you lost your mind? What are you doing?"

"That's what I'd like to know," a familiar voice called out from the audience. Michelle glanced in the direction of the voice. It was Danny! Becky and Uncle Jesse stood right next to him. And behind them stood Joe's father, Mr. Grant!

Michelle gulped hard. How was she ever going to explain this?

Chapter
15

Busted!

Stephanie gaped as Danny, Aunt Becky, and Uncle Jesse rushed onto the stage. The twins ran over to Becky, and she gathered them into her arms.

On the stage, behind her, Stephanie heard Laura murmur, "Who *are* all these people?"

"Dad, wh-what are you doing here?" Stephanie stammered. "I thought you all went out tonight."

"We did go out," Danny said. "We came to the luau!"

Stephanie shut her eyes. How could she

have been so dumb? How could she have not even considered the possibility that her family would show up at the luau?

"Stephanie!" Danny said loudly.

She opened her eyes again.

"Exactly what is going on here?" he demanded. "I thought you girls were in your room at Hideaway Haven."

"Hideaway Haven?" Amber stepped forward with a puzzled look. "But I thought you're staying here at the Hawaiian Hideaway."

Stephanie groaned. *Double* busted!

"Well, I guess I'm not staying here. Not exactly," Stephanie admitted.

"But you showed us your suite," Laura insisted.

"Your *suite?*" her father echoed. "Steph, I think you have some major explaining to do—to *all* of us."

Mahina and Lonnie stepped onto the stage. Mahina spoke into the microphone. "We're going to take a fifteen-minute break," she told the audience. "Thanks for being patient." She turned to Stephanie. "Now, what's going on with my lead dancer?"

Stephanie wished she could disappear. Instead, she smoothed down her grass skirt, took a deep breath, and plunged in.

"I wanted to tell you all the truth," she began. "I never meant to lie at all." She turned to her friends. "That first day I met you—I just came over here to look around. Then I met Lonnie and found out about the free hula lessons."

"I remember that," Lonnie said. "You didn't want to sign up at first. But I told you I wouldn't take no for an answer."

"Right. Then I met you guys, and—"

"And we begged you to join us," Amber finished for her. "Because if we didn't have at least five people, the hotel was going to cancel the class."

"I loved taking the classes. But I knew all along I wasn't supposed to be here," Stephanie admitted.

"Let me get this straight," Danny said. "This whole week you pretended that you were a guest at the Hawaiian Hideaway."

"Only to take the hula lessons," Stephanie confessed. "I'm sorry, Dad. It's just that I was really counting on doing something like this in Hawaii. And then, when we got to the Hideaway Haven, I realized they didn't offer anything like that, so . . ."

Danny crossed his arms over his chest. "I understand the Haven wasn't quite what you were counting on," he said. "But, Steph, you took a class that you never paid for."

"Excuse me." Mahina stepped forward and smiled at Danny. "The hotel pays me to teach the hula classes. And certainly their money comes from their guests. But the classes are open to anyone who wants to take them. You don't have to be a guest of the hotel to learn the hula."

"Really?" Stephanie sighed in relief. "You mean I didn't really do anything so terrible?"

"You still told me you'd be at the Haven tonight, when you were really planning to be here," her father reminded her. "And you let everyone believe you were staying here when you weren't."

"I know," Stephanie said. "And I'm sorry. It was awful, not being able to tell you guys the truth. I was always looking over my shoulder, waiting for someone to catch me."

Patricia looked puzzled. "So if you're not staying at the Hawaiian Hideaway, how did you get into that ritzy suite?"

"The chambermaid," Stephanie answered. "She helped me out."

"It was nice of you to go through all this because you didn't want to let us down." Amber smiled at Stephanie. "Weird, but nice."

"You really worked hard this week," Mahina put in. "And you're a wonderful dancer."

"I'm not quite so thrilled," Danny remarked in a dry tone.

"I know, Dad," Stephanie replied in a small voice.

"We'll discuss this whole thing further when we get back to San Francisco," he told her.

"If it's any consolation," Lonnie put in, "I think your solo was the best part of the show. I mean, before your sister interrupted it."

Stephanie had been so busy feeling guilty that she almost forgot Michelle.

"Yeah," she said. "What was that all about, Michelle? Why did you start screaming and then push me across the stage?"

"To protect you," Michelle said.

Stephanie frowned. "To protect me? From what?"

"From the Curse of the Green Lagoon," Michelle told her.

Stephanie couldn't help it. She sputtered with laughter. "Michelle, you've told some whoppers before. But this is the looniest!"

"It's true," Michelle insisted. "I accidentally swam in the Green Lagoon. I woke the evil spirit. Now it's the full moon and something really bad is going to happen!"

Stephanie blinked in surprise. "And you're actually serious about this?"

"Well, after I swam in the lagoon, bad things started happening wherever I was," Michelle explained.

"But there are no such things as curses," Danny insisted. "You know that, Michelle."

"Joe said a scientist—an *archaeologist*—told him about the curse. Archaeologists know all about this stuff."

Joe's dad pushed his way up onto the stage. "Maybe I can help clear this up," he said. "I think there's been a big misunderstanding.

You see, Dr. Matson was a guest at the Haven. One night he told me the story of the Green Lagoon."

"You mean about the treasure that's supposed to be buried there?" Mahina asked.

"Exactly," Mr. Grant said. "About two hundred years ago, a band of pirates came ashore here. People say they buried their gold and silver right on the shores of the Green Lagoon."

"And afterward they spread rumors that an evil spirit lived in the lagoon, who would curse anyone who disturbed it," Mahina finished. "In fact, they told people that the spirit had killed one of their crewmen."

"Did anyone ever find the treasure?" Molly asked.

Mr. Grant smiled. "No. About fifteen years ago—before you were born, Joe—Dr. Matson and a team of archaeologists searched for the treasure. They didn't find a thing."

Stephanie noticed that her sister still looked doubtful. "See? It's all just an old legend," she told Michelle.

Michelle turned to Joe. "And *you* believed it!" she said.

"I guess I overheard only the first part of the story," Joe confessed. "I never heard Dr. Matson say the legend was phony." His face flamed in embarrassment. "Boy. Do I feel silly."

"Yeah. I do, too," Michelle said. She frowned. "Wait a minute. If there is no curse, how do you explain all the bad things that happened this week?"

She listed everything that had gone wrong, starting with her broken sandal strap and her rash, and up to the collapsed grass hut and the broken bone at the dig.

Mr. Grant hid a smile. "I'm sure all those things had a logical explanation," he said.

"Sure. Like your rash," Danny added. "I realized today it was caused by the sunblock you used."

Michelle blinked in surprise. "The sunblock I borrowed from Uncle Jesse?"

"Right." Danny grinned. "Becky showed me the bottle this morning. It contains an ingredient that you're slightly allergic to."

"What about the other stuff that happened?" Michelle asked. "Like you and Jesse getting caught by that mysterious force in the water?"

"That's an unusual kind of riptide," Joe's dad explained. "It happens only in currents near very deep, big rocks close to shore. It's why your dad and uncle thought they were being held in the water. But that tide is part of nature. Not a curse."

"I guess I can see that now," Michelle sheepishly agreed.

Lonnie chuckled. "But why did you try to stop the show, Michelle?" he asked.

Michelle explained how she thought the curse got worse during the full moon. "I was trying to find a way to stop you from performing the hula," she told Stephanie. "Because you were the only one in our family who hadn't been affected by the curse. I figured you were next."

"But you see, I was never in any danger," Stephanie said.

"That's not true," Michelle declared. She pointed at the sandbag that hung from the fraying rope. "You were dancing right beneath that, Steph," she said. "I had to push you out of the way before it hit you."

Mahina's dark eyes grew wide. "Oh, my! It's a good thing you noticed that," she told Michelle. "Someone could have been badly hurt."

"I'll get it fixed right away," Lonnie said. "Then the show can go on!" He hurried away.

"Wow, Michelle—you actually saved me," Stephanie said. "I wish I'd known what was going on all week. I can't imagine how awful it must have been, thinking you were cursed."

"It was pretty terrible," Michelle agreed.

"And pretty funny," Uncle Jesse added. "You should have seen yourself tackle Stephanie. Totally professional. Tell me, Michelle, have you ever thought of playing football for the San Francisco 49ers?"

Stephanie chuckled. "You know, Michelle, even when you tackle me in front of an entire audience, I can't stay mad at you."

"Thanks, Steph," Michelle said shyly.

"Okay," Lonnie announced. "We're all ready to finish the show."

Stephanie glanced at her father.

"Go ahead, honey," he said. "You did look really great up there—and your public awaits."

"Thanks!" Stephanie cried. "But first I want to make sure a very important person has a front row seat."

She led Michelle by the hand. "Here, Michelle. The best seat in the house, for the best sister in the world."

*Don't miss out on any of
Stephaine and Michelle's
exciting adventures!*

FULL HOUSE™
SISTERS

*When sisters get together...
expect the unexpected!*

A MINSTREL® BOOK

Published by Pocket Books

2012-03

It's TV—in a book!
Don't miss a single hilarious episode of—

Don't Touch that Remote!

Episode 1: Sitcom School
Spencer's got his own TV show!
Watch him try to keep his wacky co-stars out of trouble!

Episode 2: The Fake Teacher (November 1999)
Is that new teacher all he seems?
And is Jay hiding something really, really big?

Episode 3: Stinky Business (January 2000)
Danny's got a brand-new career, and something smells!
Here's a clue: It ain't fish!

Episode 4: Freak Week (March 2000)
It's the spookiest show ever as the gang spends overnight in
their school.
Will Pam's next laugh be her last?

Tune in as Spencer, Pam, Danny, and Jay negotiate the riotous
world of school TV. Laugh out loud at their screwball plots and
rapid-fire TV-style joking. Join in the one-liners as this over-the-
top, off-the-wall, hilarious romp leaves you screaming—
Don't Touch That Remote!

 A MINSTREL® BOOK
Published by Pocket Books

2302